His mouth felt like fire on her lips...

Frances pushed fiercely against Ian's chest. She was totally at a disadvantage, and she knew it.

"Umm," he murmured, unperturbed. "You look like some virginal offering to the gods, lying here in the moonlight."

"Well, I don't intend to be!" she retorted, struggling to sit up. But his arms imprisoned her, and she felt the warmth of his bare skin, still damp from swimming, as he pressed against her. "Don't touch me, Ian!" she commanded in desperation.

"Oh, lay off the untouched routine," he replied scornfully. "You were waiting for me, an open invitation. But as it happens—" he got to his feet and looked down at her "—you're a bit too blatant for me, anyway. Maybe you can get some other guy to oblige...."

ROSALIE HENAGHAN
is also the author of this
Harlequin Romance

1422—THE SOPHISTICATED URCHIN

Many of these titles are available at your local bookseller.

For a free catalogue listing all available Harlequin Romances and Harlequin Presents, send your name and address to:

Coppers Girl

by

ROSALIE HENAGHAN

Harlequin Books

TORONTO • LONDON • LOS ANGELES • AMSTERDAM
SYDNEY • HAMBURG • PARIS • STOCKHOLM • ATHENS • TOKYO

Original hardcover edition published in 1981
by Mills & Boon Limited

ISBN 0-373-02462-2

Harlequin edition published March 1982

Printed in U.S.A.

CHAPTER ONE

'THE last one sounded interesting. Read it again, please, Kathy.'

The speaker, a tall, slim figure, was brushing her hair. Apparently she didn't notice the way the golden red curls sparkled; her hazel eyes were turned towards the floor where her young sister was spreadeagled, the evening paper in front of her. Kathy uncurled her long legs, held the paper out and declaimed, 'Home Help, Landgirl. Must be able to fit in with lively family. Essential be prepared to help in household tasks. Pastoral and sheep experience preferred. Position for three months, December 1—March 1. Good wages plus keep. Write to R. & J. Marsden, Coppers Road R. D. Windwhistle.'

There was a brief silence as Frances and Kathy studied the advertisements in the Situations Vacant column.

'What pastoral experience have you?' enquired Kathy sweetly, an impish grin spoiling the words.

'As much as you,' chuckled Frances. 'The only time I've been working in a paddock was the time I did that advertisement for the jeans and overall range Al Sportswear put out. I remember I had to climb on to one of those enormous harvester machines and I was scared stiff!' Deftly she pushed a decorative clip into her hair, barely glancing at the result. 'It was a beaut photo, though, Harry Smithson's a real artist with a camera.'

'Hardly qualifies as pastoral experience! Still, Sis, you are a good cook. Tell you what, if you make me a gooseberry pie for tea, I'll write a letter stating you're a great cook.'

'No deal!' laughed Frances. 'You're, incorrigible,

Kathy Elaman. Make one yourself!'

'What me?' squeaked Kathy indignantly. 'Soil my lily-white hands?'

'Yes, lazy one,' answered her sister with an affectionate glance that took any sting from the words.

'I suppose I could,' Kathy put in thoughtfully. 'Mum bought some frozen pastry the other day on special.'

'That's cheating. Mum likes to have that when she's in a hurry.'

'Hmmm. You know, that puzzles me. How can you use it in a hurry if it's frozen?'

Frances smiled at Kathy, then placed a spot of highlighter accent above her eyes.

'Wow, that looks great! I must try some too'.

'Not with my make-up, you rascal. You've used far too much in the past with your wretched experiments and last time you didn't put the tops back. Here, you can have this old lipstick.' Frances threw a small blue tube towards the figure, who caught it delightedly.

Seeing her elder sister in such an approachable mood Kathy asked,' 'Why did you leave your job, Frances? You've been there since you were twenty and that's four years ago. All you had to do was to look smashing.'

A grin remarkably like Kathy's floated briefly across Frances' face. 'A receptionist has to do more than look smashing, Kathy. I had to run the switchboard, check petty cash and handle clients as well as letters.'

'Don't throw me that red herring. Come on, why did you leave?'

'Sometimes, Kathy, a person should leave a job. You'll find when you're older that everybody has reasons for doing things which seem appropriate at the time.'

'Fobbed off again! Never mind, one day the mystery of the disappearing redhead will be solved.' Kathy's chuckle rang out at her dramatic pose.

It smoothed away the faint shadow that had darkened the lovely hazel eyes of her older sister. Kathy folded the paper again so that it stayed open at the 'Situations Vacant' column. Frances finished her make-up and studied it professionally. Her chin was a shade sharp, her nose too long, but she had learnt to minimise her faults and her eyes were lovely. One of her boy-friends had said they had reminded him of water rushing over stones, the colours changing with the light. The memory of the poetical boy-friend caused a smile, briefly showing the neat white teeth. The lips were soft and vulnerable, echoing the apparent fragility of the face. It was a surprise when she stood up to see the length of her. Looking at the fragile face, a stranger did not expect the tall lithe graceful figure that made Frances such a successful model. Her interests in squash and jogging and swimming had given her body a healthy, vital look.

She selected a flowing floral skirt in autumn tones, smoothed it on over her flat tummy, then eased herself into a new top. It was a cream lawn cleverly cut to emphasise her slim waist, the pintucked front fanning out over her breasts. Frances was not vain, but she appreciated clothes and delighted in wearing pretty garments. She tidied her room, meticulously straightening her make-up equipment, then picked up the paper.

Kathy was at her file of modelling photos and having selected one, turned triumphantly. 'Found it! Anyone looking at that would think you'd spent your life as a hayseed!'

Frances looked at the photo. It had been taken last year in the summer against a background of golden wheat, the red harvester with its solitary blue clad figure showed up magnificently. The girl in the top seat was Frances, her long jean-clad legs resting lightly on pedals. The face detail was sharp, showing the large hazel eyes and the saucy mouth.

'Right, that's pastoral experience!' chortled Kathy, doing a handstand in glee.

'You're a shocker, Kathy! It's just as well I haven't

got one with sheep!'

'Don't you want to get the job?' queried Kathy.

'Of course! But not by being dishonest' Frances said gently. Now that she had admitted it, the job sounded reasonable. Of course the family might be ghastly, but she would be able to form some idea at the interview. There was bound to be one, and considering the summer vacation of university, it could well go to an agricultural student. Still, she could at least try.

She took the paper and went down to her father's study. It was only the work of a few moments to draft and then type out an application. She was about to seal the envelope when the doorbell rang and she knew that Jamie had arrived. Her mother's voice called out, so she picked up the envelope and handed it to Kathy. 'Kathy, please put a stamp on that and run it to the box on the corner.'

'Sure thing.' Kathy plopped the letter down, the top revealing that it was not sealed. 'I'll fix it,' she said.

Frances joined Jamie, who was speaking easily with Mr and Mrs Elaman. They liked Jamie, having known him from babyhood. They knew Frances and he were just good friends and would never be any different. At the moment he was the only escort Frances would consider, and she would have been very annoyed if she had known that this date had been suggested by her mother. After dinner they went to a movie and Frances felt herself relax a little. Jamie was so easy and so understanding, she thought, such a contrast to John Brooker. Just thinking of John made her clench her fingers, making the knuckles gleam whitely. The only man she had ever met who could make her feel like a real woman, and he was married! Until she met John she had come to the conclusion that she was like a phoney store-wrapped Christmas present—all pretty glitter with nothing in the box. Well, at least she knew she could feel reaction to a man now. She remembered the day John Brooker had arrived at work. He was tall, good-looking and very charming. As soon as he had spotted Frances he had commandeered her as a guide. Work became a chance to see John, lunch an opportunity to talk, and nearly every night he asked her out for dinner. His charming smile eased his path, making his progress at work or with social occasions inevitable. Frances bit her lip as she remembered the force of his kisses and the lean attraction of his body as he held her, seeking her surrender—but some instinct held her back, making her withhold herself.

Thankfully now, Frances remembered the unknown telegraphist who had shattered her dreams. She had answered the telephone as she did hundreds of times a day. 'Telegram for John Brooker'. It was her job to take messages when the bosses in the advertising agency were out. John was outlining a multi-media deal to a new client that morning. The thought flashed through her that instant.

'I'll take the message for Mr Brooker,' she said.

The telegraphist read it out and mechanically Frances took it down. 'House sold; cash, baby and I on our way. Flight 594 Wednesday. Love you, darling, Amanda.' Routine demanded she read it back. Calmly she asked for a copy to be delivered later. She wrote her note of it and put it on John's desk. Somehow she had gone on working, her mind repeating to herself—he's married, he's married, he's married. It wasn't until the observant Mr Denby, the art executive, came by that she had been released. He had always had a soft spot for the gorgeous tall redhead at the front desk. He assigned one of the typists to cover for her and took Frances off to a nearby coffee house.

When they returned to the office an icy calmness had settled on her. She had repaired her make-up, glad that her model's knowledge helped her to disguise her feelings. Pride had helped her to greet John with apparent casualness on his return. When he had asked for messages she had been able to tell him that she had already left them on his desk. It had been much harder to tell him that she would not go out with him again. Finally she had grabbed her car keys, purse and coat and fled, glad that it was already after hours.

Routinely she had driven out of town, glad she was forced to concentrate on the heavy traffic. Finally she turned off the main road and followed a side road leading to the river. She pulled the car over to the side, shaded by the bright green leaves of the weeping willows lining the banks. The quietness of the river contrasted with the dull hum of traffic. A few curious ducks edged forward hopefully for crumbs, then realising the stillness of the tall, redhaired girl, paddled idly back to their own pursuits. A scent of rhododendrons and azaleas pervaded the air, catching her attention, finally bringing her back to herself. After a time of solitude she braced herself to go home. It had been a bad few moments telling her parents that night. They, too, had liked John and his easy charm. Now they were hurt because their firstborn had been hurt. Sensibly they had kept Frances occupied so that when Monday came the emptiness of her heart was just a slow dull ache.

The days passed. John was obviously rattled, but he had just landed a contract worth several thousand dollars, so his tenseness was easily explained.

On Wednesday he had told Frances that his wife was arriving and he would be unavailable in the afternoon. He had said it briefly, then shut himself in his office until lunchtime.

On Friday he had asked her to have lunch with him. His cool behaviour staggered Frances and she indignantly rejected him. There had been no grain of comfort in knowing she was doing the right thing. Later that afternoon she was on duty when a well-dressed, lovely young woman carrying a small baby came into the office, and she had not been surprised when she had asked to be shown to John Brooker's office. 'My husband,' she had said so softly and with so much love that

Frances was touched in spite of herself. Somehow Frances had politely wished her happiness in settling into a new city, then shown her into John's office. Strangely enough her feelings had turned to anger with John and she saw him suddenly as facile and selfish.

That weekend she had just finished a game of squash with Jamie when John came up to her. Not wanting a scene, she had climbed into John's car, determined to leave him with no doubts about her feelings. He had driven out to the beach, and Frances had noted the sharp way he had held the wheel and the tension in his face. Even so she had been totally unprepared for the force of his feelings. His passion was sincere and he told the horrified Frances that he wanted to divorce his wife. Frances told him in no uncertain terms what she thought and he had driven her home in icy silence. Her silent scorn had made her exit possible. Deep inside was growing the conviction that John Brooker wanted challenge and the more he was refused, the more he would desire.

The following week at the office had been intolerable. John seemed to be demanding more of her time, claiming that the three other typists were incompetent loons. This was patently untrue, but he reduced the poor girls to such a state they found it difficult to work. Only with Frances would he be willing to work. He asked the chief if she could be solely his secretary and Frances had been horrified. The gleam of possessive triumph on his face had only been shaken by Frances' refusal to take the position. However, she seemed to be doing an increasing workload for him. With her feelings in tatters she doubted if she could hold firm against the blandishments and charm being used so constantly. The memory of the loving face of John Brooker's wife was a reproach she could not allow herself to forget. Reluctantly she had made her decision. She had handed in her notice and worked out her leave as calmly as possible. John had ranted and raved so much she had felt sickened by his behaviour.

She wanted to get out of Christchurch and on impulse had booked a cruise for the Islands. It was something she had intended to do for a long time. Unfortunately it was not due to sail for more than three months, so she looked round for temporary employment. Fortunately her salary had been good and she had money saved, so she was not desperate. All she knew was that she wanted to get away. If John Brooker could find her easily he might continue to try to see her.

Her parents had been wonderful, thought Frances. They had supported her with their love, hiding their own anxiety. Every day the paper had been studied carefully in case a suitable position had offered. Twice Frances had been interviewed for a post, but with one man she knew she would be going from the frying pan into the fire. The second position she had applied for would have meant giving up her holiday, and she felt reluctant to do that. It was an anchor to hold on to, something colourful and bright to look forward to with hope.

She stirred in the seat. Kathy would have posted the letter to the Marsden family by now. At least there hadn't seemed any predatory male figure about that advertisement. Despite herself Frances smiled whimsically and began to concentrate on the flickering screen. The film was almost three-quarters over, but it had given her an opportunity to review the whole situation, and now she was much more at ease with herself. Jamie, hearing her soft sigh, took her hand, squeezed it gently, then released it. The odd contact touched her with its gentle care. When Jamie returned her home she had been able to thank him sincerely. They made a date to play squash the following day. For a week, day followed day in easy relaxation. Frances spent a lot of time jogging through the park near her home, the motion steadying her and the exercise doing her good. She was able to tell her mother to tell John she was out, whenever he rang. However, when the phone rang she was increasingly reluctant to answer it.

She was surprised how readily she had been able to dismiss John Brooker. Vaguely she wondered if she had been in love with him. Perhaps after all she was a cold, frigid type. She had been attracted, she could see, but not seriously tempted. The knowledge worried her vaguely and she attempted to discuss it with her mother. Mrs Elaman kept insisting that she would meet the right man one day. The old-fashioned phrase stuck in Frances' throat, but she managed to cover her feelings with a rueful laugh. 'Mum, I'm twenty-four, not eighteen!'

Kathy walked in then with the mail, a letter for Frances amongst it. Grateful for the distraction, she had read the information aloud. Her interview with J. Marsden was for the next morning at eleven o'clock. She wondered what the mysterious J. Marsden would be like. In the morning she dressed carefully. She was to have her interview over coffee in one of the department stores. That at least was something, she supposed. She wondered if the mysterious J. Marsden would be forced into drinking dozens of cups of coffee, as they interviewed prospective employees! The prospect sent her off with a smile.

J. Marsden turned out to be Jennifer Marsden, wife of Rupert. Instantly Frances felt at home with Jennifer, an easygoing, petite woman in her early thirties. She was plump with pregnancy and explained that the job was a mixture of household help, supervising her three sons, and checking stock once the harvesting season had started.

'Quite frankly, I don't care if you don't know one end of a sheep from the other, so long as we can have someone we can live with.' Her eyes twinkled mischievously. 'As a matter of fact as soon as I saw this photo I knew you were the one! My husband was impressed too. He has a similar harvester to my brother and they do a lot of contract work in summer.'

Frances looked at the photo. Young Kathy must have slipped it in. She felt a fool having to explain it, but could see the funny side of the situation. Jenny laughed too and a bond of friendship was formed.

By the time their coffee was finished Frances and Jennifer knew a great deal more about each other. Jennifer had explained that she had lost a baby with a miscarriage three years before and this time she wanted nothing to go wrong. 'My doctor is wonderful, but he's warned me that if my behaviour isn't perfect he'll whip me into hospital. Quite frankly I'd hate that as summer is such a frantically busy time on the farm, so Rupe suggested we have additional help. I was very much against the whole idea until I saw your photo. You seemed to be young and cheerful.' She paused. 'You can ride horses, can't you?' she asked.

Frances reassured her truthfully. She loved riding and had spent many hours at a stables not far from her home. As a child she had had her own pony and it had been a source of constant joy to her.

Jennifer was pleased with her answer. She outlined the hours and time off and discussed salary. It was not at all the princely sum Frances was accustomed to, but as it included her board it was sufficient for her needs. The time suited Frances perfectly too, as Kathy had pointed out originally. The life-style would be a complete change for her as it would be a welcome break from the office routine she was accustomed to in the city. She tried to take in instructions as to roads to follow to reach the farm the following Monday morning.

Happily she said, 'Goodbye,' looking forward to her new job with genuine pleasure. Back home her parents were delighted and even her young brother Martin, in his last year at High School, was pleased for her. Kathy had made a gooseberry pie for tea.

'It was to be a consolation prize if you missed out,

but it's a happy pie this way!' explained Kathy. Frances hadn't the heart to reprimand her about inserting the photo in the envelope. After all, she doubted if she would have been selected for an interview if it hadn't been for that.

It was a happy family occasion. That night when the telephone rang for her, she told her mother to tell John that she was going away.

Her spirits seemed to lift at the prospect of doing something so necessary. Once she was gone John would forget his feelings for her, and perhaps make an effort to settle with his wife and the small baby.

Early on Monday morning Frances kissed her parents a fond farewell and set off for the farm. Her suitcase was full of trousers and shorts and tops, a change from her previous working wardrobe. To drive out she had worn the pretty flounced skirt with the neat pintucked blouse. She felt quite at ease as she negotiated the cross-town traffic, then turned her car on to Yaldhurst Road. Automatically she slowed as she approached the rear of the racecourse. Some magnificent horses were already doing track work and her eyes delighted in the attractive scene. It had rained in the night, but this morning the sun had come out and the world seemed new and fresh. Frances felt cheered by this small sign.

A large plane moving ponderously in to land at the nearby airport shattered the peace with the scream of its engines. Soon she turned out on to the West Coast Road and the peaceful beauty soothed her. The smooth straight road cut its way across the flat plains seeming to stop only at the line of gigantic mountains. The Southern Alps were magnificent, standing in rugged rows of snow-tipped splendour. Around her, the patchwork quilt of the plains lay lazily spreadeagled for the sun. Crops of hay, barley, wheat, lucerne and clover showed the effect of an early, warm wet spring. Cattle moved in some paddocks, but mostly it was the sheep that caught the eye. Horses grazed and in another section she noted a pig farm. Every sign promised a good season. Now and then she passed farmhouses dotted around with trees, the fence lines linking as well as dividing. Past Hororata, a small township waiting in the sun, she turned off according to the directions Jenny had given. Her path headed more south than west towards the mighty Rakaia river. She sped along, conscious of a rising anticipation.

After driving for some time Frances saw a glimpse of an enormous old house surrounded by a wood. A glance at the letterbox told her she had reached Coppers, so she swung down the side road, knowing she was almost at her destination. Coppers was an early pioneer homestead and Frances recalled having seen pictures of it in the past. It was named for the copper beech trees that formed such a notable feature of its grounds. Even from the road the trees looked magnificent and a tree-lined drive led from the road towards the house. Frances smiled to herself. She was going to a very different type of house, judging from what Jenny had said. Travelling much more slowly now, as the road was only shingle, she kept on glancing round until she finally saw a neat, long modern house of green summerhill stone and knew she had arrived. Like its neighbour this house had been set around with trees, but here they were only small and still young. Fast-growing silver birches formed a break from the prevailing wind and Frances knew the garden would be a pleasant spot. The house had been built to get the maximum advantage of the sun. To one side a group of garages and implement sheds were screened by more trees. Frances stopped her little Mini and wondered where she should park. She smiled as Jennifer Marsden came out to greet her.

'Grand timing! My man's just arrived in for morning tea, so you can meet him. I'm sure you'll like each other. Just put the wee car in here.'

Obediently Frances drove the car in beside a big, powerful Jaguar. Her little Mini looked very small beside the big car and a Land Rover on the other side.

She grabbed her suitcase and eased out of the car. As they went into the house Jenny commented on a motor-bike in their way to the door. 'My brother's bike! Watch out for it as he's liable to leave it anywhere! He's here a lot as Rupe and he often work together.'

Now Frances was inside and found herself in a large sunny kitchen. Two men stood up as they entered, and for a panic-stricken moment Frances felt quite shy. Rupert Marsden was brown-haired, medium height and heading towards forty, thought Frances. She began to relax, sensing a quiet ease in the calm smiling face. He had a tanned outdoors look about him and he held out his hand in greeting. 'Welcome, I hope you'll enjoy your stay with us!'

Frances took his hand gratefully before turning to the other man at his side. Jennifer introduced him as her brother, Ian Burnleigh. He was a magnificent figure of a man, tall, heavily muscled, bronzed by the sun. His hair was dark brown and curly, and his eyes were a deep dark brown. He stood easily and Frances experienced a thrill of sheer animal magnetism as his hand gripped hers. 'It's great to meet such a paragon of virtue, talents and good looks: Jenny's been singing your praises.' The lazy smile took a slight sting from the words.

'I hope I live up to expectations,' she said, struggling for her normal poise.

'If you survive my three nephews for the first week of the school holidays you'll be fine.'

'Hey, don't you rubbish my sons!' chuckled Jennifer as she passed Frances a cup of tea.

Rupert looked at her quietly, then told them that Ian and he would be out most of the day. 'Jenny will show you round, have a look at the tractors, then you can ride down to the boundary. It's the river, so keep going till you reach it. There's a tank which marks one boundary and a cluster of pines and willow on the other. It's pretty straightforward. The horses are kept in the first paddock in front; you can ride the grey mare.'

'I'll show you, Frances,' put in Jennifer. 'Greytor is my horse and a beautiful lass.'

The men had finished their tea now, so they departed quickly. The roar of a motorbike echoed amid the excited barking of dogs, and Frances glanced up to see Ian Burnleigh ride off, his dog perched pillion behind him. She laughed with delight at the sight and Jenny, following her eyes, grinned too.

When Frances had finished her tea Jenny showed her to her room. Although not a large room, it was attractive, and had its own bathroom and walk-in wardrobe. Flowers had been put in a bowl on the dressing table. Frances thanked Jenny who left her to change and unpack. It took Frances only a short time to slip out of her skirt and top and pull on an old pair of jeans with a cotton blouse. There was no need for any jacket as it was already quite hot.

Together they went through the house. Next to her room was Jennifer and Rupe's room, again with their own bathroom, then the boys' rooms. Thad, the eldest, had his own room, but Ivan and Greg shared a room. As well, they had a large playroom. Two walls were lined with bookshelves which were littered with treasures dear to a boy's heart. The boys, too, had their own shower and toilet. The hall formed itself into an entrance separating the bedrooms from the living area. The lounge was a peaceful room, ranch sliders wide open to catch any faint breeze from the garden. It was not very large, but space had been given to a formal dining area. The kitchen was a room Frances approved of immediately. It had been given additional space, so a large table formed a natural centre. The latest in cooking and freezing appliances ranged along two sides. The window above the bench looked out to a swimming pool. At one end a windshield had been built partially enclosing the pool.

Frances loved the house. It was modern yet showed a simple dignity and warmth that reflected Jenny and Rupe more than they knew.

Frances and Jenny went out into the side garden. It led straight to the pool glinting openly in the sunlight.

'We love swimming,' said Jenny. Since Rupe's enclosed that end we can use the pool for much longer. As well it forms a reservoir in case we need it for firefighting.'

They moved away from the water and walked towards the big garages. A large and a smaller wheeled tractor ranged up to the jeep. Frances had once been on a school trip to a farm and remembered having a tractor ride on that occasion. Seeing her hesitation, Jenny smiled and said she would show her; expertly she started the smaller of the two machines and the noisy splutter of its motor racketed in the still air. She reversed it on to the wide parking area, then signalled Frances to open the gate at the side. When she had driven it through Frances was shown the way to manoeuvre it. Then Jenny stood down and Frances eased herself into the driving seat. She was very glad that she had a flat paddock in front of her. At least no matter which way she went she wasn't likely to hit anything! Perched up there she felt ridiculously high and she was glad Jenny hadn't pulled out the even bigger machine. Gingerly she moved the gear into first and after an initial bucking which she instinctively corrected, set off, trundling slowly. Eventually she felt braver and sped up a little. After a few minutes she knew that driving the tractor was rather fun. Then Jenny instructed her on reversing and set up a slalom course with a couple of empty boxes. She felt able when she was finished to manoeuvre the machine back to its parking place in the garage, and Jenny applauded the performance.

The horses whose paddock Frances had invaded eased themselves out of their corner and raced freely in the sunlight. Jenny pointed out Greytor and Frances studied the mare. She moved easily, with considerable grace, and Frances was pleased. Three other horses were also there, and Jenny pointed out their names. Rupe was evidently riding his at the moment. The other building Jenny pointed out was the woolshed. Ringed by stockyards, it was some distance from the house.

A glance at her watch told her it was lunch time, so they made their way back to the house. As Rupe was still with Ian and not expected for lunch the two found it easy to chat. Jenny explained that she was meant to rest for at least an hour after lunch, so she told Frances where to find saddle and bridle, to do her exploring. Frances was glad to have some time on her own. Expertly she caught and saddled Greytor, talking softly and evenly, rubbing her hands smoothly on the horse's head, easing to pat her neck, then swinging herself up with considerable style. Greytor stood quietly for a moment, then shot off like a rocket. Evidently she hadn't been ridden for a little while, so Frances let her go enjoying the mad gallop to the full. Sensing the expert rider on her back, Greytor steadied to a calm canter.

The lush pasture was bordered by a string of Douglas fir trees, then she found a stand of padiata pine. Here and there an odd clump of mixed trees patterned themselves on the soft greens of the pasture. The big grey clopped along, Frances appreciating the rhythm and the beauty around her. She was surprised to see a mob of woolly sheep close to the top paddock. Vaguely she had thought shearing would have been over.

At the gates Greytor sidled in close so she could open them easily, leaning over from the saddle. Without any pressure from her, Greytor turned sharply so she could close it behind her. Frances smiled. Even the horse knew that gates had to be closed! A sloping track led over a slight rise, then twisted itself into two. She followed one path as it led towards the direction she wanted.

Beside the path were irrigation channels. These were one of the main secrets of the productivity of the plains. Fed from the Rakaia river, the channels formed into a series of tiny dams which in turn fed the neighbouring paddocks. The sight of water made her realise how very hot it had become, and she made a note to always wear a hat in future. It was some distance to the river. She stopped to look, her eyes drinking in the beauty of the scene.

As she came closer she could see the silver ribbon braiding and looping itself over a wide area of gravel. Groups of willow lined the banks here and the river bed was broken into thousands of tiny islands, some just piles of stones littered with boulders, other covered in lupin and scrub. The Rakaia looked indolent in the sun, twinkling innocently, splitting itself into strands to seek the easiest path to the sea. Frances moved Greytor under the shade of the willows and swung off. She slipped between the bushes and clambered down a path to the river. Feeling the freshness and isolation of the spot, she breathed deeply. Her only companions were a couple of big gulls, wheeling and screeching overhead. She decided to paddle her feet in one of the streams; the water looked so cool and inviting. On impulse she pulled off her clothes, keeping on only her pants and bra. She giggled to herself, feeling deliciously abandoned, and stepped into the small pool. The iciness of the water struck her forcibly, tingling and refreshing her, and she splashed and sang, rejoicing in the splendid privacy. Then terror struck. Her foot slipped on the stones and suddenly she was vividly made aware of the danger of swimming in such a spot. One leg seemed to be jammed by a stone and a log hidden under the water. She struggled to free herself but seemed only to imprison her foot more.

The cold was seeping into her bones and she became

more frightened. Nothing had changed, yet the river no longer seemed innocent. She realised that she would have to see under the water in order to free herself. As she didn't want to wet her bra she removed it, flinging it higher towards her jeans and blouse. She bent over double in the water and struggled to lift the heavy log. Time and time again she heaved, the exertion keeping her warm. When she realised it was no good she studied the stones which held her on the other side. She smiled grimly. What a nitwit she had been, she thought. They moved easily and with a lurch she was free. She scrambled out and lay exhausted and trembling, not feeling the rough shingle. The sun warmed her gently and she was just about to replace her clothes when she saw a tall muscular figure pick them up, and, selfconscious of her near-nudity, she crossed her arms over her breasts.

'You look like a blue water baby. Here!' Ian Burnleigh tossed her the jeans, blouse and bra.

Frances sat stiffly, too frozen to move. He muttered an exclamation, stripped his shirt from his back and rubbed her dry The force of his hands warmed her chilled body and she shuddered. She pulled on her bra and blouse. He finished drying her legs and eyed her speculatively.

'Now, water baby, don't go playing in the river. It's far too dangerous for big girls.' His eyes glinted, mocking her.

Frances nodded dumbly. Somehow she should thank him, but he strode away and she was able to finish changing. To herself she could admit that Ian was a far bigger danger to her than the river. She had been shocked at the effect his touch had produced on her body. She walked slowly back to her horse, reflecting that she had been stupid. Her face had lost some of its pallor, her hazel eyes were deep dark pools. Everything she had ever learnt about swimming in rivers she had ignored, simply because of the heat of the day. To be discovered almost naked had seared her and she felt wretchedly embarrassed at the thought of having to face that cocksure, arrogant male. She climbed into the saddle, mechanically easing herself into Greytor's stride. Greytor carried her home effortlessly, and by the time she had released her she had regained some of her equilibrium. The sun had dried her hair so she slipped into her bedroom and repaired her make-up. She pulled on a cardigan as she still felt chilled, then squaring her shoulders she went out to the kitchen.

CHAPTER TWO

'Come and meet the boys,' said Jennifer gaily. 'Thaddeus, age ten, my first born, Ivan the Terrible is seven and Greg the Gorgeous is five.' The three sturdy boys eyes Frances solemnly, then Thad very correctly stepped forward and said, 'How do you do?'

Ivan the Terrible grinned cheekily and said, 'Gee, you're real pretty.'

Greg the Gorgeous just smiled. Frances smiled in return and the boys seeing the smile accepted her readily.

'I'm big now. I go to school on the bus. See, this is my bag and this is my reading book,' said Greg.

Frances dutifully admired the bag and the book. The boys had just arrived home from school. They drank the cordial their mother had prepared for them and each had a piece of cake. For herself Frances had a cup of coffee, drinking it slowly to appreciate the warmth.

The boys raced away to get into their swimming gear, stopping only for five minutes to chant their homework.

'What about you, Frances, do you want a swim?' queried Jennifer.

'Not really, thanks,' said Frances. 'Can I help with tea?'

'Not tonight! You look very tired, I hope the trip and all the touring hasn't been too much for you.'

Frances blushed slightly. She didn't want to explain her earlier escapade and the part Jennifer's brother had played. She added lightly, 'I'll go to bed early tonight. Must have my beauty sleep!'

Lying in bed that night Frances reviewed the day. Already she felt totally at home here with Rupe and Jennifer and the lads. The only worry was Ian, and she turned restlessly in her bed at the thought of him. She remembered the scorn in his eyes when he saw her at the river bed. He was good-looking, she was forced to concede, and he was much taller than herself, so he must be at least six foot one or two. A quiver ran through her as she saw again the details of the muscles in his arms and shoulders and the dark hairs on his chest. He had made his attitude plain enough—that he thought she was a cheap little tart in her nudity. Frances hid herself in the pillow, acknowledging the bad luck that he had seen her in that state. Well, she wasn't going to let him put her off. This place was a refuge for her, a place where John Brooker wouldn't find her. She pictured John in his office, but the picture kept being interrupted by a pair of scornful yet cool dark eyes set in a rugged face as craggy as the mountains.

In the morning Rupert took her round the farm. He was a good instructor, patiently showing her how the irrigation was controlled and what crops he was growing. He explained his system of pasture management which involved shifting the sheep frequently. This would be one of her jobs, Frances was told, and she struggled to learn the right names for the paddocks.

The dogs were a delight to her. The pup was her special joy. He was a frisky black ball and appropriately named Scamp. His mother, Fay, was an excellent yard dog and his father was Ian's constant companion, a black huntaway which was a good all-rounder. As well, Rupe had an old dog who made up in experience and cunning what he lacked in strength.

That afternoon Rupert had sent her down to the river on the tractor. She enjoyed the experience, gaining more confidence as she went. Jenny had waved her off smilingly. She finished the task Rupe had set, then drove steadily back. It was quite late in the afternoon when she returned and she felt hot and sticky. Frances was glad Jennifer suggested that she join the boys in a swim. She had a neat one-piece as well as her bikini in her drawer and she decided to play it safe and wear the one-piece. Her eyes sparkled as she remembered that scornful look Ian had given her down at the river.

The water was blissfully relaxing and the boys were delighted to include her in their game. Soon Jenny called them for tea.

Over tea Rupe said that the following day they would bring the woolly sheep up to the front paddock. The shearers had been forced to leave that mob the month before when the rest of the shearing had been done. Rain was still a major bugbear with shearing. The sheep had to be completely dry, and to ensure this they would be kept in the woolshed overnight.

A telephone call earlier had told Rupert that the shearers would probably be with them in two days' time.

The next day Rupert and Frances bought the woolly sheep up to the front paddock. They didn't bustle the sheep, just steadily and quietly drove them, much to young Scamp's disgust. The noon sky was murky with a line of clouds to the south and Rupert told Frances they would shed up early. After lunch Frances prepared the vegetables for tea and made a rice pudding for the boys. She vaguely noticed the build-up of cloud in the distance and was not surprised when Rupe came charging in.

'We'll have to shed up now or we'll be too late. Give Ian a ring and tell him I'll swing half the mob over to his place. He'll give me a hand. You can put these into the shed here. The boys will be home in a few minutes, so they'll help you.'

He charged off and Frances eyed the phone reluctantly. To her joy Jenny came out and she was able to pass on the message. Jenny rang as Frances fled, calling Scamp and Fay to follow.

Frances went first to the woolshed, opening the gates as she did. The yards were well kept, the posts concrete or tanalised wood. She realised that by keeping the mob to the side she could pen up much more quickly. Although she had no experience she remembered what Rupe had told her. The dogs soon had the sheep running up into the shed. Fay was a wonder dog, seeming to be in ten places at once. The two younger boys appeared on the scene: Thad had apparently joined his father. Together, they worked steadily, if noisily. Ivan the Terrible was doing an unconscious imitation of his father and Frances had to work hard to keep her face straight. When the sheep jammed up Ivan sent Fay scampering on to the top of the woolly wall, soon clearing a space. Frances went into the shed to spread the sheep evenly. That took her a long time, but she knew it was important that the sheep were not packed in too tightly. Rupe had explained it to her over lunch. Finally, satisfied, she glanced round the shed. The odour of sheep was distinctive but at this point was unpleasant. The shed was much older than the rest of the buildings on the farm. The building was not large, but it was sufficient to hold six hundred sheep. There were four big pens plus three shearers' holding pens. The gates were designed to lift up as well as sideways and shedding up Frances had appreciated their design. She was standing now along the shearing floor and could see a press and bins in the background. She was surprised at how dark it had grown and wondered if Rupe had managed to get the other mob penned safely. The boys were anxiously waiting for her to join them and she decided to drive over to help Rupe. Gleefully Ivan ran to get her keys while Greg and she headed to the garage.

It was the first time the boys had been in a Mini and they showed their delight in their questions. As Frances had not the vaguest notion as to where Ian lived Ivan and Greg both gave her a running commentary. She was glad of the distraction as it kept her mind off meeting Ian. Regardless of what she thought, it was obvious that the small boys thought he was Superman, Batman and Spiderman wrapped in one package.

Now they could see the neighbouring stockyards, and Frances drew in her breath at the sight. They seemed a vast network and the woolshed was enormous. She pulled up neatly and the boys jumped out, running eagerly to join their father. Fay had followed them and raced to Rupe too.

Glancing quickly up at the sky, Frances was aware of the heavy clouds. She joined in with helping push the sheep forward and was rewarded with a quick nod of thanks from Rupe. Lightning flared brightly as they fought to get the rest of the mob under cover. The crashing of thunder echoed in the mountains, followed by the rain. It came in great sheets, relentlessly soaking everything in its path, great plops mixing to instant mud in the dusty yards. Rupert swung the main gate down not wanting the sheep outside to dampen the dry inside. There were about thirty left out and he seemed unconcerned about those few. He asked Fran to shift them into one of the bigger old yards where some grass was growing and the sheep were only too happy to move.

Conscious of her rain-soaked body, she moved quickly, and had soon finished. She returned to the shed where Ian and Rupe were finishing penning up. She had to admire their skill ruefully, remembering her own efforts.

'You remember Frances?' Rupe said to Ian when they stood on the board again.

'How could I forget!' came the ready reply. 'Wet, water baby?' He flung her a towel and she was glad of the excuse to hide her burning cheeks.

'I won't offer to help this time,' he added sotto voce to her. His eyes held a mocking gleam as he rubbed the worst off his small nephews.

'Will you come back for a drink?' he asked Rupe.

'No, thanks, we'd better get home so Frances and the

boys can get dry.'

'O.K. I'll finish up here. See you at half past six in the morning.' Thankfully Frances ran to her car, this time Thad with her as well. Rupert had a motorbike and she heard it roar as she flicked her Mini into action. The rain steadily poured down and Frances had to drive cautiously as the wipers could barely cope. Even the boys were quiet till the top gate was reached, then a hot argument broke out as to who should get out to open the gate. They were glad to be at home. After a quick shower they sat down to a piping hot casserole. Rupe kept glancing out the window to study the clouds. When Frances queried it, he explained that the rain could cause a lot of problems if it rained very hard for a long time.

'You should see the Rakaia in flood—after a summer storm it can do a terrifying amount of damage. We have to make sure we clear the river flat paddocks. Actually Ian has a much bigger problem as his river boundary is twice the size and he has to keep a wary eye on soil erosion the whole time. However, I think this will clear in an hour or two.'

'I do hope so,' said Jenny. 'I couldn't bear shearing to be delayed again.'

It was so unusual for Jenny to sound even slightly ruffled that Frances looked at her in surprise.

Rupert put his hand over his wife's. 'Come on, love. Have a cup of tea, then bed for you. I'll look after the boys.'

'Aw, heck! Not now, Dad!' Ivan complained. 'We want to watch Superman.'

'It'll be over by seven-thirty, Dad,' said Thad with his usual good logic.

'Right! Get your pyjamas on now, then sit down quietly.'

'Dad, can I stay home to help tomorrow?' asked Thad.

'O.K., son! You're a big help to me at shearing.'

'Me too!' 'Me too!' put in Ivan and Greg.

Rupe paused. 'No—sorry, boys. Thad can. He's doing well at school, so it won't hurt him to miss one day. Ivan, your last report said you could work much harder. Greg, you mustn't miss any school, your reading is too important.'

The theme music sounded and in quick time three neatly dressed figures were sitting on the floor, eyes reflecting the wonders of Superman.

After Jenny had said goodnight, Frances quietly stacked the dishes in the machine. In this household it was a necessary invention.

'The rain's stopping, thank God!' muttered Rupert. Frances looked out. The steady thrum had died away and now only the odd spot reminded them of the cloudburst of a few hours before. Incredibly the night sky was dark but clearing fast and later the stars would shine.

The caped crusader was triumphant over the forces of evil again, so the boys were piled off to bed. Rupe read them a story, heard their prayers and tucked them up.

Frances decided to check that the sheep she had penned earlier were settling all right. She put on a light jacket, then told Rupe where she was going.

The air was fresh and cool and Frances felt refreshed jogging smoothly over to the shed.

One or two stars were peeping out and the moon, almost full, hung pale and lemon-washed in the sky, its shadowed face making ghostly figures of the dark band of trees. The woolshed stood blackly, the light-filled windows a welcome signal. Inside, all was quiet. Here and there green eyes of sheep gleamed at her in the light. She stood quietly for a few moments, then decided to check the other mob in Ian's shed. It would save Rupe time and she felt like a run. She had a pencil in her jacket pocket and found a paper in the engine room and briefly wrote an explanatory note. She placed it prominently by the door, then set off.

Frances felt glad to be running again. In the city she jogged routinely, her body needing the exercise. Here her life was full of activity, but she knew she would enjoy the run. After the intense heat of the past two days it was wonderful to feel the velvet softness of the air. She vaulted over a gate in her path and felt smug when she cleared it easily. She realised she was now on Ian's land, though she still wasn't sure in just which direction Ian lived. However, he would be occupied at his house, no doubt, he certainly wouldn't be checking stock in the moonlight. Unconsciously she stiffened at the thought and slowed her steps. However, she saw nothing but the blur of the hills and the bands of trees. It didn't take her long to reach the shed. She could see easily enough that the stock appeared comfortable. A few noisy bleats broke the peaceful quiet. There was plenty of room here as it was a much bigger shed. She glanced around automatically, noting the boards oiled and polished with the constant dragging of sheep being shorn. The long row of shearing machines hung like black skeletal arms, beyond them the sorting table, its slatted surface gleaming a dull yellow, worn with the thousands of fleeces it must have held. A big square press stood to one side and a row of bins lined another wall. In the centre was a sizeable floor space which led to a vast sliding door. Obviously trucks would be able to back up here to receive their loads of bales of wool.

Behind her the sheep moved again and she wondered what had disturbed them. She strolled over to check, unaware of the inviting picture she made to the tall figure standing by the engine room door. Once more she went to the pens, puzzled by the restlessness of the sheep. She felt herself grabbed from behind and instinctively fought. She turned to face her antagonist and recognised Ian, his hands having released her.

'You skunk, you scared me stiff!' Frances exclaimed angrily.

'Temper! Temper! My mother warned me about girls with red hair.' His eyes danced quickly. Frances felt her breath become rapid and she moistened her lips, unconscious of her vibrant beauty, red hair glinting in the dim light, her eyes dark, her whole body tense.

'You know, you look really tempting,' Ian said slowly, almost insolently, letting his eyes run up and down her body. Frances instinctively backed away and tripped over a pile of wool packs neatly stacked by the wall. Ian reached out and helped her up, the touch of his hand sending ripples of feeling along her body.

Gently he stroked the finger and thumb of her hand, tickling her palm, his eyes on her face. Frances stood still, ready to flee but oddly moved by the experience. His touch caused unknown feelings to well up, and suddenly she knew she wanted him to kiss her. As though he read the thought in her eyes he came closer and reached her to him without effort.

'Penalty for trespass,' he said softly, as his mouth found hers, stilling her tenseness. Frances found herself responding to his kiss, amazed by the vibrant attraction that flared between them. Ian's hands caressing her body, his mouth demanding, and she instinctively curled her hands round his neck, twisting the strong curly hair. A flood of desire ran through her and her body's response staggered her.

'You don't waste time, do you, water baby? Well, I've never made a sexual conquest in a woolshed before, but I'm game if you are.' His words, passionate yet controlled, in her ear, pulled her up with an icy shock.

'You're absolutely insufferable!' she cried.

'Oh, come off it! We click together. You'd be fabulous in bed, water baby! That's what you want, too.'

Ian's words cut into her sharply. Her eyes huge dark pools, Frances shook her head blindly and turned and ran. As she sped she heard his laugh echo mockingly behind her, but she knew he was making no attempt to follow her.

She didn't even remember crossing the gate or following the track home. Heart pounding, she climbed into bed, her emotions in a whirl. Never before had she reacted so physically to a man's touch. As she calmed down she was forced to admit that she had encouraged Ian, and she remembered her body's abandoned invitation. No wonder he had suggested they release their passion then! It was pure sex, she realised, with nothing of kindness or love. He had made no attempt at even pretending it was anything other than that. Gradually, still shaken, she calmed down. Somehow she had to live and work with this man. Fervently she hoped he would not be around too often. She groaned at the thought that she would see him in the shearing shed in a few hours. She knew his eyes would strip her bare, leaving her almost defenceless. The scorn in his eyes filled her with repugnance. He had made her feel cheap, something no man had ever done before. She shuddered, remembering the magnetism he had for her and the attraction of his lean hard body. She wondered if he was lying awake and thinking about her. Yet she knew, as soon as the thought came, that he would be sleeping like a log, totally uncaring of the havoc he had produced.

The morning crept in gradually. The wind had kept up in the night, but there had been no more rain. Now Frances watched the sun rise and heard Rupe move quietly down the hall. Her clock showed it was almost six.

Reluctantly she pulled herself out of bed and put on her oldest pair of jeans, then glanced at herself in the mirror. The jeans had shrunk with repeated washing and they emphasised the neat little bottom and the long slender legs. She pulled on a pale blue shirt which had been one of her brother Martin's rejects. At least it kept her covered and hid her figure. She wrapped a scarf round her hair, pulling it back from her forehead, then grinned at herself in the mirror, seeing a totally different Frances from her usual soignée self.

'Dressed for shearing,' she thought. She was completely unaware that with her hair hidden, her eyes took on an extra emphasis from the angles of her cheekbones and her mobile mouth was revealed as softly vulnerable.

Jennifer had organised morning tea and a snack, despite looking pale. Rupert told her to send one of the boys to the shed if she didn't feel well. He looked anxious, and Frances felt deeply envious of the look of tenderness he gave his wife. She was well aware of the very special love Jennifer and Rupe shared. She doubted whether she would ever find that love now. She had been searching for the man who would take her to the stars but instead, with Ian, she had seemed to land on the edge of a black hole. She finished her thought and put it away, determined to ignore him.

Two cars were drawn up by the woolshed doors. Rupe introduced Frances to the shearers, who made delighted remarks about the improvements to the scenery since their last visit.

Thad was allowed to press the button starting the machine. The heavy black leather belt which pulled the big wheel flapped sluggishly, then began to spin, setting in motion the smaller wheels above the shearers' heads. They stood easily fitting their hand pieces on to the long skeletal arms. Each one adjusted the fine shining silver combs, then, on a word, they dived into the holding pens. Frances watched fascinated as the shearer closest to her grabbed a sheep firmly, set it on its backside and pulled it from the pen on to the floor. He picked up his handpiece and pulled the rope to send his own machine in gear, in one smooth movement, then sent the cutting comb over the sheep's belly. Thad, who squatted like a hunched-up grasshopper at his side, pulled the belly wool aside and flung it into a woolpack behind him. Carefully the shearer cleared the breast and legs and head before expertly turning the sheep to shear the side. Then he bent, using a long gliding stroke from end to end. Frances had heard it called 'the long blow' and studying it now in fascination she saw the wool unfolding in a creamy richness of thick pile. At the end the shearer straightened slightly, tapped the sheep into line with his exit chute and the first sheep was shorn, its startled leap into the empty pen showing its relief.

Thad picked the fleece up in a quick but careful style, then flung it expertly on to the sorting table where his father was standing ready. He ripped the edges of the fleece off, then expertly flicked the sides to the centre, rolling the ends to the middle so it formed a neat roll. With long practised ease he threw it to the presser, who cornered it carefully in the woolpack fastened inside the press. The scene was busy yet controlled, no wasted movements, a rhythmical pattern. Frances was conscious of being the only idle person there. Rupe must have realised how she felt as he smiled and said she could keep the pens full for the shearers.

'We're lucky it's turned out fine. Ian's letting the other mob out of his shed. He'll bring them over later, or I might get you to do it.'

Frances nodded. Inside she was telling herself to play it cool with Ian. Mentally she prepared herself for seeing his tall lithe figure. She went to the back of the pens and moved some sheep into the shearers' pens. One shearer was very fast, and she realised he must be shearing a sheep in a little over a minute. When she commented to Rupe he replied that the fast shearer was indeed an expert and acknowledged as such. The pile of fleeces mounted steadily in the press in proportion to the white naked sheep bleating in the open pens. Frances was busy when Ian came in, yet she was instantly aware of his presence, the shearers' calls showing none of her reluctance to greet him. He himself seemed totally unabashed, calling out an open, 'Hi, water baby,' as he went past. By breakfast time the sweat was pouring from the shearers, and Rupe took a tally pad to count each shearer's run. Goodnatured chaffing among the friendly group went on as the men went over to the house. They ate swiftly, so they could have a laze for a short time before starting work again.

Jenny had worked hard preparing breakfast and having seen the tremendous amounts that disappeared so quickly Frances had some idea of the workload she carried. She decided to help Jenny, who was under strain, and although she put on a bright face Rupert looked at his wife thoughtfully from time to time. When Frances told Rupert she thought she should stay Rupe seemed relieved. Now that Ian was back there was really no need for her in the shed.

Frances peeled off her already smelly clothes and showered, scrubbing herself from head to foot. She changed quickly and gave her hair a quick rub. It plastered itself wetly around her scalp, but she didn't stop to dry it. She knew the heat of the kitchen would soon do that. She pulled on some well cut green slacks and a soft green blouse, nipping it into her waist with a heavy leather belt. At least now I look a bit more presentable, she thought. The blouse hugged her damp skin as she bent to put on a pair of string sandals.

'Now, Jenny, what can I so?' she asked as she walked into the kitchen.

'Well, water baby, I could suggest all sorts of possibilities,' came the lazy drawl from Ian, still sitting at the breakfast table.

Frances felt his eyes on her, taking stock of her body in detail. Then he turned back to Jenny, saying he was glad she had some help. His smile for his sister was loving and kind, and Frances had a painful glimpse of what he would be like as a husband in love with his wife. She pushed the strange thought away. She loathed this male creature who had looked on her as a means of sex and nothing else. One thing was certain, he wouldn't have the chance to touch her again. She cleared the breakfast table around him, not bothering to be quiet with the dishes, but he seemed oblivious to her crashings and bangings. She made herself busy with rinsing the dishes before stacking them in the machine. Ian left, without bothering to say anything else to her, and she wondered why that should hurt.

The dishwasher was fully loaded and she set it in motion. On Jenny's request she switched on the element and made a plate of pikelets, while Jenny buttered a date loaf she had taken from the freezer the night before. Jenny had previously cooked corned beef ready for lunch and now Frances made a start on the potatoes.

Jenny prepared two enormous baskets with tins of food, the hot pikelets still steaming and some Louise cake in neat squares. Coffee as well as tea was made, plus a water jug kept for the purpose, then milk, sugar, cups and spoons were got together.

Jenny glanced at the clock. 'Thad should be here soon to pick the baskets up. Do you think you could take one? I'm not meant to lug things and if Rupe caught me, life would be rather blue for a while.'

'Of course.' Frances had done almost a bucket of potatoes by now and looking at it Jenny laughed and said it was plenty. Their good spirits were interrupted by the sound of flying feet and Thad came running in.

'Quick, Mum, where's the grub?'

'Thaddeus! Don't you call my good food grub!' exclaimed Jenny sternly.

'Mmm, smells beaut,' he grinned at his mother unabashed.

'I've got the other one,' said Frances. She balanced the basket in one hand and the kettle in the other and with Thad walked over to the shed. As they arrived the button was pressed to stop the machines for smoko.

Frances put the basket into willing hands and fled back to the house. She had caught a glimpse of Ian's figure bending to the last fleece and she wanted to move before he made any remarks.

The day passed in a haze of meals and preparation

and cleaning up. By four o'clock Jenny and Frances were tired but glad they had coped with the meals successfully. The shearers would return to their own homes for a meal at night. Now Jenny had in a large roast of beef cooking slowly. They would have it for tea hot, then serve the remainder for lunch the next day.

Rupe came to the house to see if Frances could bring the mob over from Ian's place. She enjoyed the jaunt, glad that this time Ian was being kept busy in the woolshed. The woolly sheep were quite easy, ambling slowly towards home, and the dogs were glad of some work to do. Even the pup Scamp tried his best to moderate his enthusiasm, although he was inclined to overshoot his sheep and cause more havoc. The older dog, Fay, kept a wary eye on the situation, rather as a mother watches a child's first attempts at handling a situation, ready to step in before losing control. The leaders of the sheep knew their way and moved off, pausing now and then to reach for a particularly delectable piece of grass. They became more cautious when they realised that the woolshed was between them and their home paddocks, but the dogs gave them no choice. Ivan and Greg, now home from school, came out to join in with the other dogs, Ian's faithful black dog coming too. Dust soon stirred in the yards as the mob moved. It was too early to pen the sheep, so Frances went back to the shed to check if Rupert wanted anything else done.

Inside, the steady thrumming and whining of machinery dominated the odd bleats of sheep. Thad moved rapidly between the shearers, picking up the fleeces and flicking them on to the sorting table. A steady clicking sound made her look towards the giant press. It had been upended and now Frances watched fascinated as the two boxes' contents were compacted into one bale. Rupert and Ian were working big handles, forcing the press harder, and she would see the muscles gleaming in their backs and shoulders as they took the strain. She could see the top of the bale was held in place by a heavy wood and steel lid covered with jute sacking. Now the two men straightened and she watched as Ian put another similar lid ready, while Rupert eased the empty top box down to the floor. Ian slid it easily into position, his face showing mirth at some remark Rupe had made.

His easy grace seemed reflected as he stood there, his chest bare, bronzed and muscular, rippling in the pattern of sunshine from the skylight overhead. Frances was glad she stood with her back to the light because she knew she could not drag her eyes from his superb physical condition. A dog barked somewhere and the sound broke into her reverie, startling the thoughts that still shocked her. Ian had finished stitching the bale together and with a final whang the sides of the press split open and the fresh bale took its shape on the floor.

Ian dragged it with a powerful steel hook over towards the loading bay. He sorted through stencils and watched for a moment as Ivan and Greg carefully filled in the black insignia marking the bale with farm, number and wool classification.

Rupert came over then and said that he and Ian would shed up so she could return to the house. She fled quickly, as Ian had become conscious of her; without saying a word he had made her feel a deep physical awareness.

Back at the house she changed into her swimsuit and dived into the pool, then tired herself more by swimming energetically.

Ian and the boys dived in to join her, but she pulled herself out quickly, not wanting to run the risk of his tormenting, knowing eyes. At tea she was placed beside Ian and her appetite was banished by the feel of his muscular thigh against hers. Conversation was mainly on tallies and bales and she was interested in the discussion despite her lack of knowledge. All the same, she was glad that no attempts were made to prolong the meal; the whole household was tired and preparation for the next day still had to be made. Ian said goodnight and departed with a casual wave.

Ridiculously, Frances felt almost sorry when he had gone and she determined to make herself busy. Jenny was pleased to let her do some baking for the next day. She was exhausted when she finally fell into bed. She slept heavily until the alarm clock buzzed at six o'clock the next morning. On this second day of shearing she stayed in the house most of the day, glad to escape the noise and the dust, visiting the shed only to help Greg and Ivan with the heavy food baskets. The boys were delighted as it was Saturday and there would be no school.

On the second occasion Ian had taken the basket from her, a smile lighting his features. 'Hey, water baby, why did you run from the pool last night? Don't tell me you were scared?'

Scarlet, Frances had beaten a hasty retreat, infuriated to hear a chuckle echo her footsteps. At lunchtime she made sure she had a conversation going with the boys. Even so, Ian had come and sat beside her and her heart had fluttered like a butterfly's wings. There had not been much room at the table and he had pushed his large body hard up against hers so she could not move. She sat very straight, determined not to acknowledge the havoc his presence caused. As soon as she decently could she eased her slim figure out, smiling sweetly that she had finished.

Rupert came over to the sink where she was beginning to clear up. 'I'd like to take Jennifer out tonight to celebrate. Would you mind staying with the boys?'

'No, of course not. A quiet night is just what I want. I'd like to leave early for Christchurch in the morning.'

'Right—well, don't hurry back on Tuesday. You've done a great job helping Jenny so much and I'm very grateful.'

The shearing was finished by mid-afternoon, so the workers enlivened the occasion with a small party.

Frances had a shandy too on Rupe's insistence, but

she felt too selfconscious to be near Ian, so she excused herself, saying she wanted to swim.

Having made the statement she felt she had to carry it out. Her one-piece was a heavy material and it felt clammy on, so she ripped if off and put on her bikini. There was precious little of it, but she hoped perversely that Ian would see her in it.

Some fighting spirit made her slip it on. If he treated women like sexual objects then let him see her as one! She knew the boys were going swimming, so they would be her protection. Her eyes sparkled at the thought. For once Ian wouldn't be able to touch her.

She took two towels out and dumped them at the end of the pool, gradually edging herself into the water. The coolness was delicious on her skin. She lazed in the water contentedly, pushing out any thought. She had just pulled herself out of the water when Ian came round the side and dived in. He swam neatly down to the end of the pool, then back to where she sat on the edge.

'Come on, don't let me spoil your games, water baby.'

'You don't!' she smiled coolly. To prove it she felt she had better swim or he would accuse her of running away. She swam neatly to the other end, conscious that Ian was keeping pace with her, schooling herself to keep calm; she turned over on her back and floated, closing her eyes to let herself drift gently in the movement of the water.

'Hey, water baby, I like your bikini.' His voice about an inch from her ear startled her and she ducked suddenly, flailing one arm to regain her position. His hand neatly restrained her, and he pulled against her, his brief kisses melting her mouth.

She splattered against the water as he dumped her and she splashed him in a fury of silver sparkles. He laughed and sent a spray of water showering her in return.

The boys arrived then and joined in splashing gleefully, Ian and Frances making a team against the assaults of the three small figures. Finally she surrendered, climbed out of the pool and lay exhausted on the towel, covering herself modestly with the other one. Her gesture caused a gleam in Ian's eye and seeing it she pulled an extra layer of pride around her. The towels had been given to her by the manufacturer after she had used them in a magazine advertisement. She rubbed the soft fluffy pile absentmindedly, remembering the series of poses she had worked out with the photographer. That would really give the sex-mad creature behind her something to think about!

Deliberately she decided to teach him a lesson. Knowing he was at the end of the pool and she was in full view, she raised one shapely leg. She bent forward, apparently casually, to dry the leg, gradually easing it down and rubbing her body in slow sensual movement with the towel from ankle to thigh. Tantalisingly slowly she moved her other leg and repeated the gesture. She turned her face to the opposite side so she could control her grin before turning back to the pool in apparent dewy-eyed innocence. Now for the finale, she thought grimly. Up till now she had kept the other towel round her top, hiding her slim figure. She flipped it away, arching her body so her breasts stood proudly. Her buttocks she pressed harder into the side of the concrete, knowing this would pull in her tummy muscles and make her waist seem even smaller. She raised her arms with the towel and wrapped it neatly round her hair. Still apparently casual, she stood up and calmly did a model walk away from the pool, deliberately pushing her hips forward to accent the wiggle in her posterior. She held her head high until she regained her bedroom, where she laughed uproariously. There, that should fix him! she thought mirthfully. She showered and changed into a neat long silk patio dress in lemon and gold. As she changed she caught sight of her glowing eyes in the mirror and felt slightly ashamed of herself. Perhaps she hadn't been wise to tease Ian. She dismissed the thought hurriedly and applied some cool perfume.

In the background she heard the roar of Ian's motorbike. Evidently he hadn't stayed long in the pool after her act, she realised, a cheeky glow glinting again. In her imagination there had even seemed to be an angry throb to the machine, and her eyes lit with laughter.

CHAPTER THREE

FRANCES went out to the kitchen and began preparing an enormous pot of chips for the boys. Jennifer and Rupe said goodnight. They looked a charming couple going out together. Jennifer wore a dark blue calf-length dress with three pleated tiers that skilfully minimised her pregnancy. Her hair was curled softly about her face and her big dark eyes were highlighted. Rupe wore a formal suit and he looked the epitome of the country gentleman.

The boys were delighted with the chips and steak and side salad Frances had made. It had been so uncomfortable sitting beside Ian at lunch and tea the night before that Frances was hungry too. The boys helped her clear away the dishes and they watched television for a short time. Thad was just about asleep on his feet and Ivan and Greg were usually tired by this time, so she sent them to bed. She read them a story, tucked them up and said 'Goodnight'. Greg curled his arms around her for a goodnight kiss and she felt warmed by his loving gesture. Thad was already asleep when she went to check and Ivan the Terrible looked soft and cuddly and defenceless. His eyes grinned sleepily as she ruffled the dark curly hair so much like his uncle's.

There wasn't anything she wanted to watch on television, so she sat for a while in the dark quietness, then decided to play some music on the stereo. She listened to a record, only vaguely letting it permeate her consciousness.

It was very hot still. Idly she thought of having another swim, but if the boys cried out she knew she wouldn't be able to hear them, so reluctantly she abandoned the idea. It was far too early to go to bed, but she could at least get into her nightwear. It would be much cooler. As no one was around she slipped on a satin two-piece which left her midriff exposed. She picked up a kung-fu style wrap-around satin jacket that matched it and went to check the boys, All three were sleeping peacefully so she walked back to the lounge.

'How do you manage to look so provocative all the time?' Ian's voice lazily amused, drawled out the question.

'Ian, what are you doing here?' Hastily she wrapped her jacket round her scantily clad figure.

'What a greeting! I've come to see you, of course.' He eyed her satin-clad body and Frances wished her jacket covered more than her bottom.

'You've got great legs, water baby,' he said.

Frances spoke tartly, 'Thank you. I'm afraid I wasn't expecting visitors.'

'Weren't you? Somehow this afternoon I got the impression there was an invitation somewhere.'

Frances struggled with embarrassment and decided that she should at least offer him a cup of tea or coffee. However, he turned them down, going instead to the drinks cabinet.

'I'll get you a drink.'

'Fine, very light on Bacardi and plenty of Coke, please.' She sat on the floor by the stereo and flicked through the records. Earlier she had inspected them, but it gave her time to control herself and quieten her heart, which seemed to be beating painfully quickly. She was very much aware of Jennifer and Rupe's absence and the distance of the lounge from the boys' bedrooms. She was relieved to see the door to the passage was wide open.

Ian brought her a drink, toasted her and stood by the speaker. He turned up the music, then went to shut the door.

'Don't want to wake the boys!' he grinned. 'Come and dance.'

Frances liked dancing normally and the rhythm of the record was a very strong beat. Ian danced opposite her, the disco sound obviously one he enjoyed. Frances began to relax as they danced, losing her fear as he led her gently but expertly. She began to enjoy herself and forgot her earlier tensions. At the end of the record they collapsed laughing on the couch, and Ian's unexpected touch made her stiffen immediately. He went to the record player and put on an old-time dance record of soft romantic mood. They listened to it quietly for a while then Ian stood and pulled her into his arms. They danced slowly round the floor, the music weaving its soft melody around them.

Gradually she nestled closer to Ian, letting the music draw them together, only the gentle but firm pressure of his hands guiding her caused sparks of physical awareness so that she trembled in the warmth of his arms. A thousand danger signals ripped through her as he claimed her mouth, drowning her in a torrent of feeling as he eased her on to the thick rug. She caught him to her, answering his passion with an abandoned invitation, but he turned from her, casually reaching for his drink on the small table. Calmly he stood up and switched off the music.

'I think that makes us even in the sex games stakes. One love to you this afternoon, but the game to me tonight!'

His eyes gleamed as he took in the picture she made, lying in an agony of confusion. With a sob Frances jumped up, hating this male creature who had played her so expertly.

'You—you beast!' she spat at him, turning to flee.

He gripped her arm, forcing her to face him. 'Women!' he muttered. 'You don't like your own tactics used against you, do you? Now don't get angry, water baby. I can satisfy you any time.' He crushed her against him, making her aware of the hard solid wall of flesh of his body entrapping her with his strength. She struggled to free herself as his mouth took hers, kissing her brutally, a kiss with no love or tenderness.

The sound of dogs barking and a car's engine shocked them both and instinctively Ian released her. Frances fled, shutting her bedroom door behind her, as though she could thereby shut out the memory and feelings of that evening. The knowledge of her response to Ian was a bitter blow. What strange chemistry made them react to each other this way? she wondered. She wept softly as she remembered his taunting remarks. If only she could have held herself aloof, she thought. Then a grim smile forced its way out. It would have been easier for King Canute to have stopped the tides, she realised. The same man whose attitude to her was so cheapening was the same man who was idolised by his three small nephews, loved by his sister and her husband and, from comments she had heard, generally well liked by others around him.

She herself had seen him tenderly taking a soot from Greg's eye, comforting Ivan after a bad fall, teasing Thad and treating his sister with a gentle love Frances envied. He worked hard on his farm, Frances knew from comments Jenny or Rupe had made.

If only he wasn't Jenny's brother, she thought. How could she continue to face Ian after what had happened? Should she give up the job? Reluctantly she decided she couldn't hurt Jenny so badly. Several times during the week Jenny had been so kind and thoughtful, charmingly grateful for Frances' efforts to help. Frances felt trapped. She couldn't let Jenny down at this late stage. Well, at least she had the weekend in town to work out a plan to keep out of a certain man's way.

CHAPTER FOUR

EARLY the next morning Frances dressed for town, putting on tights, petticoat and suit, which felt strangely unfamiliar. She made herself some breakfast and tiptoed along to Jenny and Rupe's room to see if they wanted any tea. Jenny lay snuggled into her husband, his arm outflung in a protective gesture. Silently Frances tiptoed back to the kitchen. How wonderful to be loved like that, she thought. She had always dreamed that one day she would meet a man, fall in love, marry and have children. Her lips twisted wryly. She had certainly met a man who puzzled and disturbed her, yet to her he showed nothing of love, she acknowledged.

She sped away from the farm, swung on to the main road and headed the car back to Christchurch. It seemed incredible to think so much had happened in just a week. She had barely time to think of her family or even to wonder about John Brooker and his wife. Strangely enough she felt a little more sympathetic towards him. Now she had experienced a passionate unfulfilled yearning it had taught her a little more of human needs.

Determinedly she thrust the thought of Ian from her, seeking relief in driving steadily and easily. The quietness of the countryside calmed and soothed her, and when she reached down she drove straight to the little city chapel she loved. It was dim and restful and the atmosphere of prayer helped her, She knew now that she had been partly at fault, regretting that she had teased Ian with those sexual poses by the pool. She remembered, too, how he had found her on the riverbed, almost totally naked, apparently giving him the belief that she cared little for conventions. Only now, when she had nearly lost so much, could she admit the truth. She wanted Ian, she realised, not as a casual animal passion but as a constant companion who would love and cherish her. After the service she met some friends who invited her for morning tea, but she explained that she wanted to get home.

What could she answer to her mother's anxious, 'How did it go?'

'Marvellous,' she answered quietly. After all, she could hardly blurt out, 'I'm in love.' Her secret was too newly discovered for that. Besides, there was no chance of that love ever being completed.

'My dear Frances, life on the farm seems to suit you!'

Kathy pirouetted round her sister. 'You've got that vim feeling, that zest for living,' mimicking the television advertisement. 'Hey, Sis, what are the boys like?'

'Nothing like you,' was Frances' answer as she ruffled her sister's hair. 'Where's Dad?'

'He's gone to get Aunt Kate for dinner. They should be here soon. Martin's at the beach with friends.'

Kathy pulled her sister's case in from the car. 'Gosh, it's light!'

'I didn't bring much home,' laughed Frances. 'I'm only here till Tuesday morning.'

Her sister's rueful expression told her how sharply young Kathy had missed her. Perhaps it might be possible for Kathy to come out to the farm one day. The Christmas holidays would soon be on them with their six weeks of freedom from school.

'How's school?' she asked Kathy.

'Hmm, O.K., I guess. I got the results of my language and social studies exams and they weren't too bad. I've got maths and science this week, so I've been studying.'

Frances' father arrived then, bringing Aunt Kate for the family meal. There was much merriment in their home. Frances realised how good it felt to be accepted unquestioningly. They lingered over the meal, Aunt Kate keeping them entertained with a string of family jokes. Sunday afternoons were generally relaxed affairs. Frances followed Aunt Kate's example by resting. Later she gave Kathy a game of tennis and much to that young lady's delight they were both hard-fought matches.

As they walked back home Kathy said jokingly, 'You must be in love, your tennis is lousy!' She beat a hasty retreat as Frances ran after her, and Frances was left thinking that young Kathy was far too perceptive. Thank goodness she would have these two days to recover herself before going back to the farm.

Over tea she told them about life on the farm and in particular the shearing. Kathy decided it sounded great fun and was quite disappointed that her elder sister had helped with the catering rather than in the shed.

'It's not fair! Why do girls have to do the cooking when they could be doing exciting things like shearing?' Kathy muttered indignantly.

Mr Elaman jokingly said that if Kathy really wanted to try, many shearing gangs were employing women and some women were extremely good. Kathy was greatly impressed; already she had declared she wanted to be a politician when she grew up, although she hadn't decided which party to follow! There was a deal of goodnatured chaffing about Kathy being the world's first champion lady shearer—the family well knew that Kathy was not the most inclined to do any physical work!

'Telephone for Frances,' sang her mother.

Wondering who it would be, Frances ran to answer it, and was pleased to hear Harry Smithson who took most of her modelling assignment work. Harry had been asked to do some large stills for a window display for the New Year. Harry was a member of the advertising agency she had worked with, but he did a number of private clients' photographic work as well. He explained that he had tried to contact her earlier but with no success. Her mother had told him that she would be back at the weekend.

'Sorry it's not much notice, Frances. It's mainly summer casual range and they want a country backdrop. We'll pop up to Victoria Park. I've got two other girls as well.'

'Sounds fun. What do I wear and what time do you want me?' queried Frances.

She had worked often with Harry and one of his studies of her had won him considerable recognition in his own field. Harry was a professional to his fingertips, and he reeled off the items she was to bring and then gave her explicit directions. As well he told her the fee she would receive, and that certainly was an incentive! She would be pleased to see Harry as he could tell her about her friends at work and he might even mention how John Brooker was getting along.

The morning dawned fine and clear. At ten o'clock Frances drove up Hackthorne Road, past the stone castlelike structure of the Sign of the Takahe, turned sharply and swung up on to the road leading to Victoria Park. She reached the top and parked in the area beside Harry's van and another car. Immediately she took her gear and headed to the area Harry had mentioned yesterday. She walked across the park, which was practically empty. A gardener was mowing the lawn, the tractor pulling a wide mower behind it. Frances admired his skill as she lightly followed the track past the children's playground. Normally a hive of active movement, the giant wooden climbing frame, swings and stepping stones stood abandoned, only a mass of angles and lines. She passed a ragged old macrocarpa tree. From one of its sturdy branches hung the tattered remains of a rope for a Tarzan swing. Tantalisingly it was swaying slightly above her head and instinctively she reached for it.

Then she climbed the hill and gazed about. Harry and the other two models were preparing the shots. She waved in recognition and Harry hugged her gleefully.

'Great to have you along, Frances.'

They chatted with comfortable ease. Frances had worked with the other girls before. One she knew quite well, having worked with her before on numerous occasions. Harry soon started lining up frames and angles and then work started in earnest. In front of them the city of Christchurch lay spilt on the ground from the sweep of the coastline marking the giant estuary in the east to the flat green paddocks of Halswell in the west.

Instinctively Frances looked towards the towering mountains that met the sky in the north. Her eyes picked out Mount Hutt, its top snow-covered. From this angle she knew exactly where Ian's farm lay. Lovingly she allowed herself to dream of what it would be like to be loved by Ian, to be cherished and needed.

Harry's voice penetrated her consciousness. 'That's swell, honey, keep that romantic yearning look—hold it, fantastic, baby; right arm up—great, terrific! That's it! Relax!'

Frances ruefully pulled herself together. She noticed Harry looking at her a trifle oddly, but it wasn't until the other girls had left and she was helping Harry pack up that they had time to chat.

'Well, Frances, do tell Harry!'

'Tell you what?' she enquired meekly.

'Who is he? Don't tell me the rumour about John Brooker and you was true? Is that why you left?'

Frances fielded the questions neatly, diverting attention from John Brooker by saying she was working on a farm and how much she enjoyed the change. Harry realised that Frances was in love, but he also knew it wasn't John Brooker who was involved. He had sighed with relief because he was fond of Frances and he knew her high moral standards. When he heard the rumour about John and Frances he had refused to believe it. They dropped the topic and went on to discuss other workmates, and it was only hunger that made them both laughingly aware of time. Harry followed Frances to her home, where Mrs Elaman cooked them some tomatoes for lunch. Finally Harry said farewell, anxious to get back to his darkroom to check his work.

Frances felt strangely elated to be driving back to the farm. She looked forward to seeing Jenny and Rupe and the boys. She had determined to ignore Ian, hard though that might be. She knew she would not be satisfied with a mere physical relationship, so she would do her best to keep out of his way. Even thinking of him was a strange pleasure, she recognised, but for her a dangerous one. For she knew so little about him. A thought struck her suddenly—perhaps he was married. She tried to recall what Jenny had said about him. However, she had heard no mention of any wife and she was sure the boys or Jenny would have mentioned it. Now she recalled hearing about Gam, a strange name certainly, but she knew she was an elderly relative who lived with Ian. Perhaps Jenny would tell her more.

The road was becoming more familiar already. She stopped only briefly in town to buy the boys some sweets. With being so many miles from any dairy they were not accustomed to the pleasure of candy, and Frances remembered Kathy's delight when she had bought her some novelty sweets before. Accordingly she bought three bags of fudge, half a dozen large gobstoppers and some whacky false teeth which turned out to be marshmallow and peppermint. She knew the boys would be delighted.

Jennifer was at the door to greet her when she arrived. 'Kettle's on!'

'Grand, I need a cup now. My goodness, it was hot driving out!' Outwardly composed, Frances picked up her bag and carried it into the farmhouse. Once inside she was reassured by the silence. Obviously Rupe and Ian were not there. She changed quickly, then rejoined Jenny in the large sunny kitchen.

'The men are down at the river. They've been working non-stop, so I threw a wobbly this morning and made them have a break!' Jenny grinned cheerfully, her eyes dancing with amusement. 'Ian's been like a bear with two sore heads and Rupe's heading for a heart attack if he doesn't slow down. So I threatened them. I'd turn into a nagging woman if they didn't have the day off.'

'Why didn't you go too?' queried Frances.

'I'd have liked to if I wasn't so preggie,' Jenny chuckled. 'However, I'm happy having a rest from housework. I've given Rupe instructions to catch a salmon, so I hope he does.'

'What about Ian? Does he like fishing?' Frances asked lightly.

'Yes and no. Most of the time he prefers his boat. He took it down this morning. It's a jet boat,' Jenny explained, seeing Frances' puzzled look.

'How super! They look madly exciting the way they skim over the water.'

'Have you ever been for a ride, Frances?

'Never—I'd love to experience it.'

'I'll get Ian to take you one day. It's great fun exploring a big river like the Rakaia. I think the best part is the Gorge where the cliffs rise so steeply. Actually Ian's quite keen on exploring the major rivers of the South Island. He's already done several from mouth to source. You should get him talking about it, he's quite entertaining on the subject. If he ever gets married I hope his wife will like boating and rivers or poor old Ian will be confined to the Rakaia!'

Jenny continued chatting as Frances drank her tea. Well, at least she knew now that Ian wasn't married, and the knowledge warmed her.

They put the dishes into the machine and Frances helped prepare the vegetables for dinner. 'Let's go and give the garden a shock,' said Jenny. 'It's far too nice to spend time inside.'

Frances found some gardening tools and some old gardening gloves. The gardens were Jenny's delight, and in a few years when the trees were mature it would be even better. One or two gums planted well back from the house were quite big already and a row of silver birches lined the driveway. There were a lot of specimen trees too, which were slower growing, and Frances recognised liquid ambers, limes and walnut as well as several copper beech trees. In one corner was a very unusual copper beech, and Jenny acknowledged her interest. 'Yes, it is rather special. A weeping variety—or if you want the full botanical splendour, fagus sylvatica purpurea pendula!'

'Heavens!' chortled Frances, 'the name's bigger than the tree. How do you remember them?'

'Well, I suppose I picked it up as a child. Gam is nuts about trees and of course Mum and Dad were keen too. Growing up at Coppers, trees form such a natural surrounding I would be lost without them. You haven't been to Coppers yet, have you?'

'Is that where you grew up? No wonder you know the trees' names! It looks a magnificent old homestead from the road.'

'You're right, of course! But I look at my nice modern house and know I'd rather have it. Cleaning Coppers is a real drag.' Jenny laughed, surprised to see the look on Frances' face.

'I love old houses—I can't agree with you, Jenny. There's so much character in old houses you can't get in modern homes.'

'Phooey!' snorted Jenny. 'You try keeping house in one of them for six months and see how much you appreciate character then! Plus all the maintenance work Ian has to do! One thing I will concede, the rooms are much larger. Our bedroom would be about the size of Ian's dressing room. My ancestors had grandiose ideas of space! Ask Ian to show you his bedroom.' Her eye caught Frances' blush and the two laughed delightedly! 'No, on second thoughts that wouldn't be the right thing, would it?'

Privately Frances agreed with her. So many puzzling things fell into place. As owner of Coppers Ian would have considerable appeal for women who would see him as an eligible bachelor. Add to that his extraordinary good looks and his animal magnetism and Frances mellowed slightly in her attitude to him. He had been plagued by women, she guessed, and he had obviously written her off as one chasing after him prepared to use any feminine wiles. She seized a healthy dandelion and pulled at it, glad to be able to hide her blushing cheeks. She decided to keep to her original idea of keeping out of his way. It must be more important than ever. With a final heave the dandelion gave way and she flipped over on her back. Jenny and Frances both laughed and cunningly Frances diverted her with a question about Thad, knowing Jenny would only be too happy to talk about her sons.

After lunch Jenny went for her rest and Frances went on with the gardening. She worked steadily and felt pleased with her efforts by the time the boys came home from school. They were overjoyed with the sweets she had bought them and wanted to ride down to show their father their wonderful new false teeth. Frances helped them saddle their mounts and admired their youthful skill. They waved a cheerful farewell and turned their horses towards the river.

Peace descended again, so Frances went inside and prepared tea. She had seen some gooseberry bushes in the garden and had picked quite a sizeable pile of the small green globules. Deftly she whipped up some pastry, scalloping the edge neatly. With the pie in the oven she went and showered, slipping into a cool cream linen dress. She had a copper brooch and bracelet she liked to wear with the dress and fastened them on. Her hair glistened as she clipped it firmly back from her face. She would deliberately hide her crowning glory, she decided. She wound a strip of emerald green silk into a turban enclosing the sparkling gold. Suddenly she decided not to wear the copper jewellery. Ian might connect it with some desire on her part to be noticed. She took it off and stared at herself in the mirror. Well, she had done her best not to look seductive, she thought, blissfully unaware that her eyes now reflected the green of the scarf and that her figure in the superbly tailored dress appeared slim and lovely.

She went out to the kitchen and removed the pie from the oven as the boys came running in, tumbling over the doorway like a group of puppies. 'We had a ride with Uncle Ian!' said Greg, getting the first word in and kissing his mother rapturously as she laid the table.

'I drove it, Mum,' said Thad proudly.

'It's not fair! Uncle Ian said he could drive it because he worked so hard when the shearers were here. If Dad had let me stay home I would have been just as good,' Ivan whined.

'That's enough of that, young man!' His father, hearing his complaint, spoke sternly. 'Wash first, then dinner! Oh, Ian, there's plenty here if you want to stay.'

'Fine. I must admit, Sis, that I'd enjoy eating here tonight. Can I smell gooseberry pie?' Ian smiled at his sister.

Frances turned away. The last thing she wanted was to face Ian. She beat up some cream, deliberately making the task take a long time so she would not be forced into joining the family group. Unfortunately the cream was in danger of being over-beaten before she heard Rupe and Ian slip down to the bathroom!

At dinner that night she carefully joined the three younger boys on one side. Jenny suggested Ivan sit beside his uncle and his good temper was restored by this singular honour. For Frances the meal was not a relaxed one. She was conscious throughout of Ian's presence opposite her and to lift her eyes to face that enigmatic gaze required considerable courage. Oddly enough she enjoyed receiving his thoroughly boyish praise for the gooseberry pie. After the meal she helped Jenny tidy up, then excused herself to write letters. Jenny seemed a little disappointed, but Frances was determined not to intrude. It was significant that it was Ian's presence that made her feel like that.

She said goodnight to everyone generally and went straight to her room. She wrote a letter to Harry to give him her address, then sealed and stamped the envelope. She slipped into the hall to put it on the mail table; the boys would put it into the letterbox in the morning.

Slowly the evening passed. Frances would have liked to have gone for a run in the cool night air, but she was determined to stay inside. Her bed seemed to be the only place to go, even if it was ridiculously early.

In the morning Frances helped Rupert clean up the woolshed. It was hot and dirty work all day and she was conscious she had never looked and smelled so horrible in her life. She had a lengthy shower, scrubbing herself thoroughly and washing her hair until her scalp tingled and prickled. Knowing Ian was not expected, she put on a soft blue dress with the copper jewellery and was rewarded with Ivan's, 'Gee, you look nice!' She stayed up to watch television, Greg curled up in one corner, his elder brothers having taken themselves to bed much earlier.

'You smell nice,' he whispered quietly, and Frances cuddled his slim form closer. When he fell asleep beside her Rupe gently picked him up and carried him to bed.

'Tomorrow we'll have a party here—oh, just ourselves and Gam and Ian, of course. We celebrate the end of shearing. The trucks come tomorrow to take the wool away, so it's the end of a lot of work. We all dress up and I cook a special meal and it's rather fun!'

Rupert and Frances went round the sheep together in the morning. He showed her again how the irrigation worked and watched as she manoeuvred the peg into position. Confident she could manage that, they went round the paddocks, Rupe pointing out factors to watch.

In the afternoon Frances helped Jenny prepare some of the delicacies for the meal. Already the goose was simmering gently in the oven and neatly wrapped in shining foil lay a generous portion of smoked salmon which had been frozen earlier. She set the formal dining table, making tiny sprays for Gam and Jenny of miniature pink rosebuds and fern. Happily she found a crystal bowl and filled it with tiny flowers, arranging them to form a neat low ball with the green fern forming a delicate tracery.

When the boys arrived home from school they hurried through their homework and did their chores quickly before their swim. Afterwards they climbed into their Sunday best shorts and shirts and, faces gleaming, hung round the kitchen appreciatively sniffing. Finally Jenny threw them into the lounge to watch television while Frances and she changed. Jenny wore the pretty dark blue tiered dress and Frances selected one of her old favourites, a silky-soft green-toned dress. Its tiny ribbon straps led across her shoulders, the bodice was fitted to the waist, the skirt flaring gently to mid-calf. She hadn't worn it at the farm, although she had used it regularly in town. It took her longer than usual to dress; perversely tonight she really wanted to look beautiful. She selected an old pendant with a fine gold chain and placed it in position. It was an exquisite piece with aquamarines and seed pearls which had belonged to her grandmother. She dressed her hair into an upswept style with deeply curving curls around her face swooping into a waterfall of curls at the back. When she had finished dressing she felt a small pride in knowing she looked as nice as possible. It gave her confidence that she could spend the evening in Ian's company without spoiling it for Jenny, Rupe and the boys.

As she walked out to the lounge an appreciative

silence greeted her appearance.

Rupe came over and took her to meet Gam. It was easy to see the relationship to Jenny and Ian in the tall, brown-haired woman. She spoke quietly to Frances, explaining that Gam had been her title for years. 'I'm actually Thad, Ivan and Greg's Great-Aunt Matilda, but that's rather a long name for small children! Their grandfather was my big brother, and he was a real darling of a man. I was very much of a surprise gift to the family and was spoilt outrageously. When I finished at university I went overseas, met Ricardo and lived in Italy for twenty years. When Ricardo died I came home to Coppers.'

'And thank God for that,' said Ian, approaching them with a drink for Gam. He enquired what Frances would like to drink, and politely poured her a dry sherry. When their hands met over the stem of the crystal glass Frances stiffened involuntarily and knew Ian saw her reaction. Deliberately she turned away from him and questioned Gam about life in Italy, a subject she hoped Gam was happy to talk about.

The meal was superb—first the apple and orange juice, followed by an oyster cocktail and to the delight of all the smoked salmon served with a creamy tangy sauce and the main dish, the big goose, bought steaming to the table. The three little boys were wide-eyed with the splendour of the feast and with being allowed a taste of the various light wines. The meal was pleasantly entertaining. Gam was a natural raconteur and she told many stories of previous 'wool away' occasions. As well, she kept them all laughing with highlights of her recent trip to a conservationists' conference, gently mimicking the characteristics of several well-known folk. It did not hide her deep knowledge and love of her pet field, and now that she knew Gam's surname Frances recognised her as a nationally known lecturer on trees and conservation.

The three boys were obviously a special delight to her

and she questioned them about the coming holidays. Frances caught a conspiratorial wink from Jenny as the boys discussed their favourite beaches. By the time the dessert of lychees was reached, plans for a holiday at Kaiteriteri beach were well advanced, much to the delight of three brown-haired boys. Gam had arranged a holiday house for three weeks from the eighth of January for herself and the boys. Only small Greg looked slightly anxious at the prospect of such a lengthy time away from his parents. He looked at his big brothers, who were so delighted at the prospect, and turned back to his plate with a worried frown. His uncle Ian, who had been observing him, said, 'Greg, what if I come up and see you for a couple of days?'

The smile that lit the face was ample reward. His beam shot from ear to ear; everything would be all right if Uncle Ian was going to come and see them.

Frances had to admit that Ian loved his family and they loved him. He was wonderful with the boys, playing with them yet always fairly, assessing their capabilities with skill and judgment. With them he was quickly compassionate and full of fun.

CHAPTER FIVE

After the meal Rupe and he cleaned up, insisting that Gam, Frances and Jenny had earned their rest. The three boys helped, then were taken off to bed by their beloved Uncle Ian, going willingly because he was reading them a story.

They had coffee and a liqueur and Frances felt pleasantly mellow. Gam was so likeable it wasn't necessary to erect barriers against her, and Frances spoke of her family and friends. When Rupe and Ian rejoined them Jenny suggested dancing and Frances, unaware, went pale with horror at the thought. Rupe put the record player on and played a popular soft mood piece, pulling his wife into his arms despite her laughing protests. Ian danced with Gam and Frances was heartily relieved that she wasn't having to dance. Then Rupe came and danced with her, thanking her for her assistance with Jenny. When Ian asked her to dance she hesitated, unwilling to go into his arms when she knew their traitorous power. However, it was abundantly clear he was doing it out of some sense of duty and, unwilling to spoil the happy occasion, she agreed. She could not relax and knew she was dancing badly, her thoughts muddling her concentration and missing the beat. Ian obviously was infuriated; she had danced so easily with him before and now she was a miserable non-rhythmic stiff bundle. His eyes gleamed as he looked at her and she turned away. They were both glad when the dance was over and she was reclaimed by Rupe, much to her great relief. Now that she had coped and the evening was almost over she moved softly and easily against Rupe, feeling relaxed and unafraid. After the dance she excused herself, politely saying to Gam that she had enjoyed meeting her.

'I hope we see a lot of you in the future. Come over and see me later on, perhaps next week?' said Gam.

She said goodnight to the others and nearly missed Ian's quiet voice saying, 'Want me to read you a story, water baby?' before she fled.

The next morning Rupert called Frances. 'On Monday Jenny has an appointment with her gynaecologist in Christchurch. Normally I'd go with her, but I'm hoping to get organised with the hay machines over the weekend and start on Monday. It's early, but the first cut can usually be made before Christmas.' He grinned. 'Jenny's going to throw a wobbly, but with the baby coming in January we'll have to go to town for a while, so we must get ahead while we can! The weather's been obliging, I must say.'

Later Frances was glad she had been warned. Jenny's normally cheerful countenance paled when she heard and obviously recognised the sound of the big red machine. She threw the potato knife down and still clutching the potato went marching indignantly towards the garage.

Frances smiled at her wrath and wondered how it would turn out. It was some time before Rupe and Jenny returned to the house. Later Frances wondered aloud what had happened to the potato, but Jenny's grin was unabashed. Rupe laughed too and kissed his wife passionately. 'Peace, peace,' she answered. It was an old formula and a happy one thought Frances as the three worked out details for harvesting.

It was only when she was in bed that she realised that she never did hear the end of the potato and her lips twisted wryly. She enjoyed being in Jenny and Rupe's company. It was good to see a marriage which was working, both sides loving to give as well as take. Her own parents had been similarly blessed and Frances felt a pang of regret that she could not analyse. Her dream of Ian loving her and cherishing her was so sweet that she didn't want to wake the next morning, but the noise of the boys dressing for school soon took her out of bed.

On Saturday she drove home again for the weekend, and as she went past Coppers she deliberately thumbed her nose at Ian's house, sleeping in its magnificent setting of old trees. The childish gesture put a smile on her lips that remained over the weekend.

On her return on Sunday night she came back to an empty house. Jenny had left her a note telling her to drive over to Coppers on her arrival, if she wanted. Evidently they were spending the evening there. Frances was determined to stay out of Ian's range, and although she would have loved to have seen Jenny's former home she certainly had no intention of visiting there now. She sat in the cool of the garden, swinging idly on the lounge seat under the silver birch. It wasn't much later that the family arrived home, the boys tired and sleepy.

In the early morning Frances checked the stock and irrigation on her own. This would be her principal task now that harvesting was starting. Everything was normal, much to her relief. Ahead lay the great spread of the river and she eased Greytor down to the shingle, letting the horse drink in one of the many tiny streams. The heat was trying already and she paddled her feet, but was not tempted to do more. Then she climbed back on Greytor and they cantered rhythmically back to the house. Frances arrived back at the house for morning tea and hastily showered and changed into town wear. Jenny was waiting for her and the two women were looking forward to the time in town. Frances dropped Jenny at the clinic and arranged to meet at Ballantyne's for lunch at one o'clock.

She drifted in and out of shops, stopping to buy the boys some more sweets and a novelty candy necklace for Kathy. In a small gift shop she saw some exquisite hand-rolled silk scarves. One was in pink and deeper pink tonings and Frances knew it was just what her mother wanted. She eyed it dubiously, not liking its price, but then remembering the cheque for the modelling she decided to purchase it. It would make a splendid Christmas present. The salesgirl wrapped it neatly in tissue and Frances was pleased with her choice.

She wandered over to the cosmetic section, having decided to buy Kathy some lipstick. Earlier she had been to the theatrical suppliers and bought some stage make-up as her Christmas gift to her young sister. Kathy loved dressing up as a clown or a Black and White Minstrel, and both Mrs Elaman and Frances had suffered the loss of make-up from these occasions, so she knew Kathy would be delighted with her Christmas present. She selected a soft pink she knew Kathy would suit and having paid for it set out for Ballantynes. She had bought Martin a jersey and her father a new tennis racquet, an item he had been talking about for months but never done anything about.

Frances walked along Colombo Street and crossed the Square. The red tiles sounded under her high heels tapping quickly as she walked. She glanced about, as familiar with the scene as the pigeons and the seagulls waiting for scraps—the Regent Theatre with its attractive plasterwork and dome, the old Post Office which people were trying to preserve. The big gothic style stone Cathedral had just been repaired and its spire pointed heavenwards, contrasting its quiet dignity with the modern high rise buildings opposite. Frances stopped at a colourful fruit barrow and bought Jenny some rich ripe cherries.

Many folk were buying their lunch and had perched themselves round on seats or steps ready to be entertained. The well known black figure of the wizard declaimed in one corner, opposed in another corner by the diminutive figure of the Bible lady playing her violin. Many well dressed office workers had drifted out to the Square, enjoying its pedestrian areas.

A glance at the light clock above the Insurance building hurried Frances' footsteps. She crossed to the side and joined the crowds on the footpath. Soon she entered Ballantynes large department store and met Jenny in the lounge by the restaurant. They enjoyed the smorgasbord provided and the cool air-conditioned comfort after the heat outside. Frances was delighted to hear Jenny's excellent report from the doctor.

'You must have worked the miracle! My blood pressure has gone down, so at the moment there's no risk of having to be hospitalised. It's made a big difference having you around.'

'Well, you pay me for the privilege,' chuckled Frances.

'I know, but you do a lot more than you have to, it's more like having a young sister around the place. Rupe says you're trying very hard on the farm and the boys think you're wonderful. We really will miss you in March. By the way, Gam thought you were a rather special person too.'

'I'm afraid your brother doesn't approve of me,' said Frances, smiling.

'No, you're right—Ian has a thing about models, unfortunately. He's been impossible lately. Still, I'm sure he wouldn't be rude.' Jenny's eyes darkened anxiously, as she looked at Frances.

Frances quickly tossed off a wry, 'I'll keep out of his way!' before changing the subject.

They spoke for some time on the subject of Christmas presents, and Frances delightedly showed Jenny the exquisite scarf.

Idly Frances glanced around. A couple had just taken a table a few seats away. She watched as the man drew out a chair for the girl, his hand lingering on her bare shoulder exposed by the blouse she wore, and Frances drew in her breath sharply as she recognised John Brooker.

Jenny followed her gaze. 'Handsome-looking guy,'

she said lightly. 'One of your beaux?'

'I used to go out with him,' Frances admitted. 'Then I found out he had a wife and baby, so I finished it!'

'What a skunk!' said Jenny. 'Thank God I've got Rupert. If he played around I think I'd go crazy. Come on, let's get going. He's quite put me off having any more.'

Out into the sunshine again they went. Jenny and Rupe had ordered a canoe for Thad and today was a good opportunity to pick it up. Greg was going to get his wish for a proper horse, his pony according to him being too slow. Ivan was to get a leather saddle and his old one would be passed on to Greg's new horse.

'It's complicated, making thrifty use of things, yet making sure everyone has an equal chance of something new,' explained Jenny. 'I'm buying Rupe a lilo bed for the pool—he won't be the only one to use it, though,' she added with a grin. 'As for Ian, I'm stumped. I'm determined not to buy him shirts or socks. Have you any ideas?'

Fleetingly, Frances thought of several, all unmentionable. She grimaced and thought of Jenny's mentioning Ian's boat. 'Is there anything he'd like for his boat?' she asked.

'Frances, you're a gem! I know exactly what he wants. Rupe mentioned the other day that the spare life jacket is in poor shape, so I'll buy him that. I might get him something else at the sports shop too.'

They took the car back to the sports shop and lingered over the racks of interesting goods. The staff loaded up the canoe and the other items as they made their way back to the car.

'You know, I just can't face driving back into that heat,' said Jenny. 'Let's go into Hagley Park and get cool. The car's like an oven; at least we can park it under the trees till it's cooler!'

They drove away from the shops, crossed the river and headed towards the museum shortly afterwards.

They turned off the road and entered the drive of big trees that led the way into the heart of the gardens surrounding the museum. The car from the side window looked like a modern version of Santa Claus' sleigh, so they locked it carefully before heading over the footbridge across the Avon. A small trout could be seen as a dark shadow against the stones. Some ducks were back-pedalling against the current so they could stay in line with the bridge, hopefully waiting for passersby to throw scraps. Realising Jenny and Frances were empty-handed, they ceased their efforts and paddled off to investigate elsewhere.

Once over the bridge they walked to the shade of a nearby Camperdown elm which Frances remembered. Under its capacious branches was a cool space that Jenny was delighted to find. There she could lie comfortably without worrying about the idle glances of others. 'I must remember this tree again. We used to have one at home, but Ian and I used to keep pruning it by piling in and out so fast. The poor tree took a long time to recover. It wasn't such a beauty as this magnificent specimen, though. We had a giant ash we made a tree hut in, though, and we still decorate it on Christmas Day. It's enormous fun all round. We go to church at midnight, then have supper, and in the morning we go back to Coppers. I usually give Gam a hand, then we decorate the tree. This year I won't be doing any tree climbing,' she twinkled, 'just supervising!'

After a half an hour's rest Frances was pleased to see Jenny's colour was back to normal. She walked over to the nearby cafeteria and bought a couple of soft drinks, which they sipped while walking slowly round the grounds enjoying the beauty of the trees. Jenny was an expert guide, knowing all sorts of fascinating things about the different specimens. Seeing Frances' interest she regaled her with the botanical names, explaining the original references, and the whole garden was made much more interesting by her comments.

Seeing the swings and slides reminded Jenny of the boys at home and she looked at her watch. 'I suppose we'd better get back home. It's been good having your company.'

Frances drove the powerful car back to the farm. At the beginning she had been a trifle scared of the big silver machine after her nippy Mini, but she soon adapted and revelled in the power and acceleration of the Jaguar. Soon they were heading towards Coppers and Jenny instructed her to turn in.

'I'll leave the Christmas presents here. If I hide them at home the boys will ferret them out in no time. A canoe and a saddle are not the easiest things to hide in a modern house.' She smiled briefly. 'Besides, you must see Gam. She was disappointed you didn't come over the other night.'

Frances was busy negotiating the sharp angle turn from the main road into Coppers drive. The old trees had grown so tall the outer branches almost formed a tunnel of green. She followed the gravel-lined drive as it snaked its way towards the homestead finally opening out into a parklike vista with the house on the rise. It was a two-storey weatherboard structure, obviously colonial in its sturdy strength, steep roofline and dormer windows. It lay peacefully in the sun surrounded by its green lawn, a band of bright dahlias in one corner. The house was painted white with facings of green and a deep grey roof. The northwest corner had a large turret peeping skyward above a round-shaped cantilevered window.

Frances felt her heart beat faster. The house could have been the house of her dreams, welcoming her in the sunlight. She drew in her breath sharply, struggling to appear composed. As she stepped from the car the noise of dogs barking brought Gam out to meet them. Together they lifted the canoe out and deposited it in the garage.

'Ian can put it and the saddle away later—let's have a drink.'

'I must ring the boys and tell them to do the potatoes and carrots for tea,' put in Jenny. She entered so casually that Frances was forced to follow, curious in spite of herself. They sat down in a sunroom-type porch filled with shelves containing beautiful pot plants. Gam returned after a moment with a tea-tray and Frances couldn't help but notice the fine bone china of the tea-set. She was enjoying herself as Gam explained some of the history of the house.

They were just finishing their tea when the sound of a farm bike could be heard. Frances steeled herself to act naturally when Ian walked into the room shortly afterwards. However, she couldn't help but grin at his appearance; he looked filthy from head to foot, with grass stuck to his curly hair and shirt. His eyes were ringed with red and looked sore.

'Apologies for being the original hayseed,' he joked.

'Did you start cutting the Big Flat today?' queried Jenny as she poured her brother a cup of tea.

'Yes! And we finished it too!' he added, obviously pleased. 'We'll do Rupe's south river flats tomorrow and then cut over here.'

'Come over for a swim later,' put in Jenny.

'I might do that. I've still got some bookwork to do, but I've been putting it off so long another day won't matter. How did you get on at the doc's?' Ian asked.

'Fine. Both well!' Jenny grinned.

'That's a relief at any rate. I noticed the saddle and canoe for the boys out there. I guess you want them hidden for Christmas?'

'Please, Ian. Now I must get home.' They said goodbye and went out to the car. Frances eased herself into the driver's seat, acutely conscious of Ian's glance. She prayed she wouldn't grind the gears in front of him and was relieved when she manoeuvred the car quite neatly. She concentrated on driving the car, resolutely putting out of her mind the picture of the man she had left behind.

Jenny said idly, 'You must go to see Gam one morning, she'll show you over the house.'

'I'd like that. The sunroom is super.'

'I'd still rather have mine,' Jenny laughed merrily. 'It's just as well, isn't it! I know quite a few of my friends like old furniture and so on, and Ian's nuts on antiques, by the way. He's always on the lookout for bits and pieces.'

They arrived home then, and the three boys rushed out to greet their mother. They were very pleased with themselves as Greg and Ivan had peeled the potatoes and Thad had prepared carrots and cabbage. It was not long before dinner was sizzling on the stove. Rupe was showering when they arrived, and Frances realised that he was probably just as tired as Ian.

After tea she pulled out the sweets for the boys and they were overjoyed at the unexpected treat. They went off to bed and she settled down with a book. Rupe had made his wife go to bed straight after tea and they sat companionably as Rupe entered up notes in his farming log.

'I thought Ian might have been over for a swim,' put in Rupe. 'Doesn't look like it now. I'll probably have one soon—it's hot, isn't it!'

Frances had been longing for a swim, but after the last occasion she was determined not to be seen in the pool by Ian. She realised it was eight-thirty and twilight was just closing in, as Rupe had said; obviously Ian must have changed his mind. She changed into her bikini and slipped into the pool. The water struck cold against her warm skin, but once she adjusted she realised that the pool temperature was quite warm. She stretched out and floated lazily, letting the water lap against the side of her body. A contented smile drifted across her face. When a slight splash rippled across the pool she thought it was Rupe joining her and opened her eyes lazily, taking time to adjust to the twilight.

'Hi, water baby!' murmured a soft deep voice inches from her, and with a gasp Frances reacted. She choked on the water and Ian patted her on the back apologising for startling her.

'You looked like a water nymph floating like Ophelia in the twilight.' He lifted her up, easily putting her on the edge of the pool. He proceeded to swim a few lengths while Frances recovered herself. Finally he too let the water hold him and he glanced over at her. She was acutely conscious of her near-nudity and slipped into the water.

They swam together, not speaking, yet each aware of the other. There was a bitter-sweetness for Frances about the swim, as the sky darkened and the first stars glinted. It was something of an anti-climax when Rupe joined them, shattering the fragile mood. They swam together easily now and it was almost as though the earlier antagonism had gone. After ten minutes Frances realised she was getting cold, so she hauled herself out and ran to get changed. She showered briefly as the hot water for once had run out and she was made even colder by the cold shower. As it was the summer she had no warm nightwear, so she put on a jacket over her pretty white nightie and slipped into bed. She debated whether to make herself a cup of tea, but she had heard Ian and Rupe talking there, after her shower. One thing she did not want was for Ian to see her in her night attire again. She shivered and sneezed, realising that her hair was still very wet. She looked at her blow dryer, shivering, but she was too cold to move.

A knock on the door sounded and she heard a teacup rattle, as she called, 'Come in.'

'Rupe told me to bring you one. I've just taken Jenny one.' Ian stood there and handed her a steaming hot cup of tea. His glance took in her frozen form and wet hair and he walked into her bathroom and grabbed a towel. He waited until she finished the tea before drawing her cold body against his, his hands towelling her hair dry.

'Stupid little water baby! Look at you! Even the boys would have more sense.'

He rubbed fiercely at her hair, until the blood ran again in her scalp. Weakly she thanked him, and he threw the sodden towel in the direction of the bathroom, picked up the empty tea-cup and swung out. Frances lay in bed, very shaken by this treatment, until she realised that he would have done the same for anyone. Grimacing ruefully to herself, she turned over and slept dreamlessly.

The household rose early, the boys getting themselves dressed for school while Jenny prepared breakfast. Frances had put on a pair of green shorts and an old tee-shirt and her hair glinted in the light. She had brushed it hard that morning as Ian's drying had left it a mass of tangles. Ian arrived as they were finishing breakfast, and apart from a glance which flickered over her, he had ignored her and spoke quickly to Rupe about the work in hand. Frances was glad to be able to escape to the farm. She walked to the garage and lifted the familiar saddle, blanket and bridle to the horse paddock fence.

Greytor stood quietly, letting her come up and slip the bridle over her head. She strapped it up, then spoke softly to Greytor as she led the grey mare to the fence. She straightened out the blanket, placing it carefully, then lifted the saddle into position. It was only a few minutes later that she rode round to the garage to check with Rupe on the last instructions. She listened closely as he explained what she had to do, unconsciously making a pleasant picture as she sat Greytor easily. Ian waited quietly as Rupe said farewell, so she waved a hand in his direction.

She had to shift one mob of sheep into a neighbouring paddock and as it was the first time she had done it on her own she was hoping she would manage easily. The dogs gambolled and frisked beside her, Scamp and Fay running ahead. Frances felt quite ridiculously pleased when two of Ian's dogs joined her. However, they abandoned her on hearing the roar of Ian's bike, so she was left with just Fay and Scamp. Greatly to her delight young Scamp helped round up the sheep and they went through the gate as Rupert trundled past on the big tractor. He waved and she acknowledged his presence with a ready smile, pleased that she had everything under control.

Frances completed the shifting and shut the gate behind her carefully. She cantered on down to the river and was relieved to see most things in order. Greytor knew when she turned her head for home that they were almost through and she sped up. There was a fallen tree in the way and she jumped it instinctively. It was only about two feet high and Greytor cleared it with plenty of room. Frances leant forward and patted Greytor; evidently the horse had been jumped before. When she came to the gate she was tempted to jump it, but decided she had better check with Jenny first. Greytor was such a lovely easy horse Jenny wouldn't like to be told she'd been jumping fences without checking!

When Frances reached the house Jenny had smoko ready for her to take to the men. She gave her a quick drink before she packed the thermos in the saddlebag and tied the food bag on too. Greytor seemed surprised at having to go out again, but she submitted patiently and they rode down to the south river flats.

The hay paddock was being cut steadily, as neat bands fell from the machine. The big machine trundled slowly along and Frances watched as Ian turned it at the far fence. It gobbled its way steadily towards her and Greytor moved restlessly, not liking its relentless approach. Frances swung herself down and flung an arm round her neck, and Greytor nickered gently. She unstrapped the bags and deposited them by the post, then expertly flung herself up on to Greytor again. Both men looked grimy already and she noticed they both had goggles on today. Rupe waved as she lifted her hand, then rode back to the farm. Behind her she heard the machine stop and was glad she had cleared off so quickly.

Once she arrived back at the farmhouse she removed Greytor's saddle, looped her bridle round her neck and led her back into the horse paddock. Later, she knew, she would have to ride down with afternoon tea, but poor Greytor wouldn't relish having the saddle on for so long in the heat.

Jenny had set the table for lunch and was busy cutting up a salad. Frances washed herself, then started on vacuuming the bedrooms, knowing that Jenny found that difficult. Shortly after twelve the men rode back on Ian's bike, and she felt a quick pang of sympathy for them. It was very hot and sweat had made tiny muddy paths down their backs, which were reddened by the sun. Jenny insisted they wear hats in the afternoon and both nodded that they would.

Ian sat opposite Frances and she deliberately contributed to the conversation, determined not to let Ian's presence throw her. It was more difficult than she knew, for his very earthiness seemed to touch a primeval instinct in her. She was glad when they left straight after the meal and her heartbeat could settle into a quiet rhythm again.

After lunch she cleared the dishes and sent Jenny off to her rest. It was extremely hot and she decided to have a swim now rather than later. After half an hour in the warm water she changed into her shorts and top again and prepared the smoko thermos. She put on a big sunhat to protect her from the glare. A glance at the temperature had told her it was twenty-eight degrees, and as she rode to the hay paddock she felt increasingly sorry for Rupe in the heat. She told herself she didn't feel any sorrow for Ian; he deserved his discomfort, she thought tartly. They had just finished one line as she pulled up, so they stopped immediately. There were no trees in that paddock, so they stood in the shade of the machine and drank thirstily. Sweat glistened on their bare skin covered with grime, their goggle marks made strange white rings around their eyes. Both wiped themselves thankfully on the towel Jenny had wrapped round the thermos. They were too hot to say much, contenting themselves with drinking the hot tea. Frances stood patiently waiting to take back the flasks. Rupe told her they would be late back for tea. 'Tell Jenny to put on extra for Ian. Gam's away again, so he can eat with us!'

Ian's eyes flicked at her, his face wearing a slightly mischievous look rather like Ivan the Terrible's. He knew her discomfiture only too well, so she abruptly pulled her sunhat forward to disguise the colour she knew stained her cheeks. After ten minutes' rest they gave her the now empty containers and climbed back to their machines. Greytor carefully picked her way across the sharp stubble, pausing here and there to snort as the flying dust struck her smooth velvet nostrils.

On her return the boys were running homewards from the school bus. Despite the heat they were full of enthusiasm to ride down to the flats to see the work in progress. All three were loud in their disgust at having to change first and having to have their homework checked before going. All three disdained shirts and sped out to their horses. Frances heard the shouts of frustration as Greg's fat old pony, full of cunning wisdom, resisted Greg's attempts to catch him.

Evidently the pony had decided it was too hot a day to work and as soon as Greg approached one side he sped to the other. She was about to go to help him when Thad hauled his small brother up in front of him. Even from this distance Frances could hear Greg's efforts at telling his pony what he thought of such behaviour. She smiled despite herself and went back to the house, where Jenny too was glancing out the window at the scene, Greg clutching Thad's horse, the two small bodies moving to the motion. Beside them Ivan the Terrible made mock charges, veering away at the last moment, his high spirits very evident.

Frances passed on the message Rupe had given her and Jenny nodded. 'They'll probably go on till last light. Would you like to wait for your dinner or have it with the boys?'

Frances eagerly said she would rather have hers with the boys. Their father sent them home at six o'clock so after unsaddling their horses they had a quick swim. They wanted Frances to join them and she was only too happy to do so. Jenny too sat on the edge dangling her swollen legs into the pool. It was fun splashing and diving with the boys. At length their movements slowed, so Jenny sent them to shower. The boys put on their pyjamas, but Frances put on a pale blue shirt-waister of fine lawn. She set her hair deftly, then went out to tea. Afterwards the boys went to bed and Frances watched television.

It was almost nine o'clock before the men returned, tired, dirty and hungry. Frances was glad she could watch television in peace as Jenny went to dish up dinner. Later she was smiling at the antics of a comedian when Ian came up to her.

'It's a change to see you with dry hair!' he laughed. His finger curled round a soft tendril and he watched as it sprang back to her head. 'Going swimming? It's moonlight,' he said.

Shaken, Frances shook her head. Ian stood there, his towel carelessly flung over his powerful shoulders, his trunks fitting him neatly. He turned away and Frances returned to the programme, but had the greatest difficulty in following it suddenly. After some time Rupert and Jenny said goodnight and she was left in peace. It was still very warm. She had the ranch sliders open and decided to walk in the garden. Oddly she had been hurt that Ian hadn't said goodnight to her. She reminded herself that there would only be hurt in the relationship and with a sigh she turned off the television set. She walked out to the garden, then went towards the back. The bright stars seemed to hang like a golden mobile in the sky. She sat down by a patch of honeysuckle, drawing in her breath at its scent. Relaxed, she laid back her head, reaching up to pull down one of the flowers. Idly she sucked the nectar, and closed her eyes.

'Sweets to the sweet.' Ian's mouth on hers lifted away the honeysuckle. Startled by his appearance and the fire of his mouth, Frances pushed at him, knowing herself totally disadvantaged.

'You look like some virginal offering to the gods, lying there in the moonlight.' His eyes were very dark and the light played strange tricks on the angles of his face.

'Well, I most certainly don't intend to be!' Frances answered with asperity. She struggled to sit up, but his arm imprisoned her as he studied her slowly. She felt the touch of his bare skin, still damp from his swim, as he leant against her and kissed her. Painfully she iced herself against his touch, remembering with bitterness the last time he had kissed her. She eased away from him, getting to her feet in a quick lithe movement. 'Don't you touch me, Ian!'

'Oh, lay off the big act,' he snorted. 'Don't give me that untouched routine. You lie in wait for me out here, carefully out of sight of the house, but right by my bike. I've never been known to turn down an invitation like that.' He stood up casually and moved to his bike. 'As it happens, it's a bit too blatant for my taste. You happen to be employed here and I don't want Jenny and Rupe upset. Get some other guy to oblige.'

He kicked the motor into life and roared off, while Frances gazed stupidly after him, her mind still staggering from his cruelty. Blindly she made her way back to the house, cursing the impulse that had made her walk in the moonlight. She wished she had seen his motorbike, but it had been hidden in the shadows of the tree.

In her bedroom she cried bitterly, her agony searing her. It seemed that every time Ian saw her alone she caused him to see her as a tramp. He took it for granted she was used to sleeping around, she thought, with an icy shock, hearing his scornful recommendation again. What had caused him to have such a cheap view of her sex? she wondered, with a new womanly intuition. She did not know how to handle the situation, she realised dimly. If only his touch didn't set her senses reeling! Even the thought of his kiss sent her body thrilling with delight. Chagrined, she punched the pillows, wishing it was Ian's body she was hitting. The thought of Ian sitting quiet under attack made her laugh hysterically, and she pulled herself up short. She would just have to keep out of his way and make sure they were never alone. As the long night dragged on she tried to reconcile the Ian she saw with Jenny, Rupe and the boys with the Ian she knew. It was a horrible sensation to know he had no respect for her and one she was unfamiliar with. The fact that he had totally misread the situation was small consolation. It was dawn before she fell asleep into a tormented dream in which Ian was curtained off by a vast chasm that yawned perilously at her feet.

The children's noises as they made ready for school wakened her. She dressed neatly in denim shorts with a blue tee-shirt, tucking it into her shorts and slapping her big leather belt round her waist. She was not surprised by the appearance of her face. Her cheeks seemed oddly shrunken and her eyes seemed twice their size and deeply shadowed. Desperately she grabbed her make-up, trying to cover up the despair in her face.

She went out to the kitchen and was startled that Ian was there already. Unsteadily she poured herself some tea and ate a piece of toast, knowing she would draw a comment if she didn't. She knew Ian was looking at her, his face shuttered, and she forced herself to listen to what Rupe was telling her. Rapidly she excused herself, for once leaving Jenny with all the dishes, but she knew she couldn't sit opposite Ian, feeling his glance pulling her to pieces. She saddled Greytor and galloped towards the back of the farm.

Halfway there she altered the irrigation as Rupe had shown her, then she slowed Greytor's pace, not wanting to blow her. She went on down to the river, checking the mob she had moved earlier. Idly she noticed that the fence by the river needed fixing and made a note to tell Rupe. She was late getting back to the house, perhaps subconsciously not wishing to take the smoko down to Ian. Seeing Jenny struggling down to meet her, she felt guilty. However, Jenny insisted the walk was appreciated and Frances smiled as she handed up the bags. She tied them on loosely and cantered away, her hair tossed by the wind into shining, sparkling flashes of copper and gold. The men saw her coming and switched off as she approached. Rupe took the refreshments from her and she told him about the fence. He shook his head ruefully and he said he would slip down on his way home. Ian did not approach her, but waited stiffly by the tractor. Frances turned Greytor and rode away holding herself proudly. As though Greytor sensed her mood of frustration she galloped quickly, and the tension began to drain from Frances. She was unaware of the picture she made or the eyes of the tall man following her, their expression puzzled.

Back home she released Greytor and gave her a solid rub-down. She decided to either jog down or take the car in the afternoon as it was hard to keep the horse yarded in the heat. Back at the house she showered and changed, then helped Jenny with the washing.

CHAPTER SIX

DAY followed day in a haze of heat. First Rupe's, then Ian's hay was cut and harvested. Fortunately for Frances Ian didn't come over to use the pool in the evening. After their own hay was done the men went contracting to nearby farms. The boys finished school and they eagerly went with Rupe and Ian when they could. Frances went round the stock, shifting the sheep as Rupert said. She wondered how Ian found time to do his own work, but occasionally she saw him riding round his farm.

The heat was enervating and she had no appetite. She knew she was losing weight from the fit of her clothes. Her leather belt could now be done up two notches tighter. One day she borrowed Jenny's machine and ran in bigger darts on her shirts and shorts.

Jenny smiled. 'Here, if you lose any more weight, we won't be able to see you!'

Francis told her that she always lost weight in summer and Jenny nodded. 'Guess so, but seriously, Frances, you're not eating. Is anything wrong?' She was able to answer lightly, reassuring Jenny, but after that she tried to eat a little more. At the weekends she went home, where she could relax and summon her defences in case she would need them against Ian. However, he seemed to be away contracting most of the time.

Gradually she began to relax, as she learnt the routine of the farm. Now she could tell when the pasture needed a rest or the stock had to be shifted. At least she knew Jenny and Rupe were pleased with her and even to herself she admitted she was working hard. Jenny wasn't keeping very well and Frances regularly took her to the clinic, enjoying their 'town days'. Sometimes the boys came with them and they enjoyed these jaunts as she tried to get them there in time for the eleven o'clock movies.

Several times she visited Coppers. At first she had turned down the invitation from Gam, but seeing Jenny's puzzled look she accepted the second. After that she went willingly, thoroughly at ease with Gam, but only when she knew that Ian was miles away contracting.

One day Jenny asked her to take the rest of the Christmas presents over while the boys were with their father. She drove down the tree tunnel, as she had named the drive, and swung into the now familiar yard. Gam helped her unload the presents and showed her into her own sitting room.

'You've never seen all through, have you?' said Gam as they had the inevitable but welcome tea. 'When we've finished I'll take you round.'

Gam's sitting room was on one side of the house, where she had her own completely self-contained flat. It was furnished with much love and style, elegance of line being of natural importance to the older woman. She had a small kitchen, bathroom and a lovely sunny bedroom. The kitchen opened into the sunroom porch which both Ian and Gam shared. Now she walked into the main part, entering a kitchen which seemed quite modern in its appliances. Its oak cupboards bespoke an older age, though, and she marvelled at the size of the pantry and the former scullery which had been turned into a cool room. From there they went into the dining room. It had a lofty ceiling with highly ornate plaster work resembling Grecian dancers. The table could seat at least twelve and the glow of the deep wood was beautiful. The old chairs were ornately carved and padded firmly. A fireplace with colourful tiles was in the centre.

From there Gam lead the way into a wide hall. It was dark, with a sweep of stairs, again heavily carved, leading upstairs. The handrails had been worn to a shiny old gold with the many polishings over the years. Gam was delighted to find such interest and explained that her grandfather had befriended an early settler who was expert at carving. 'He made the chairs in the dining room and the stairs in the hall. Actually they're well worth studying. He came from Scotland, but his wife died on the voyage coming out here. She died giving birth and the baby died too. He never got over it, unfortunately. He drifted out here and stayed. Apparently he thought my grandmother was like his poor dead bride; she was Scottish and she had red hair too. When they started building he started making the stair supports in his spare time, and in his old age he made the dining room chairs. If you look on the back of the chairs you'll see a fern leaf design surrounding a bud of a thistle. The same motif is done on each step rail.'

'It's lovely,' Frances exclaimed. 'What happened to him?'

'Ah well! I wonder if I should tell. You see, he used to drink fairly heavily, so my grandfather told him he'd pay his passage back to Scotland if he'd stop drinking. He did stop and my grandfather took him to the boat. The boat sailed past Spain and my grandfather got word that he'd been lost overboard.' She paused. 'My grandfather knew that was where his wife and baby had been buried at sea all those years before. Perhaps the memory of that was too much for him, or perhaps he just had too much to drink, or maybe it was one of those unfortunate coincidences. But we remember him, at any rate.'

She led the way into a room off the hall. It had a heavy rolltop desk and shelving covered with stock books and agricultural magazines. One wall was a bookcase. A lot were old, but the last four rows were modern titles. Frances made no comment, feeling an intruder into Ian's study. She backed away, there was too much of Ian's personality in the room. Gam smiled suddenly, 'Come into the main room, it'll cheer you up. Stupid of me to tell you of past history.'

'Oh no! I was most interested, Gam.' Frances followed as Gam led the way into the lounge. It was a spacious room with a high ceiling, again, like the dining room, richly decorated. Large windows, which were a much more modern addition, let in plenty of sunlight. The room had some lovely pieces of furniture as well as a velvet suite and velvet curtains. The fireplace was of king-size proportions and the solid mantelpiece was a remarkable piece of timber in its own right. Frances couldn't resist smoothing the wood under her hands. At each end she found the tiny carving of the fern and the thistle. The fireplace was set ready for a match, yet the room had an air of scarcely being used. Inside herself, Frances knew that Ian would feel lonely in this room. It was built for a family, not for one man. No wonder Ian used his study and the sunroom.

The sunshine poured into the room as she stood there imagining it full of people and flowers. It had such an air of graciousness and she tried to explain it to Gam.

'Hmph! Ian's last girl-friend thought it was ghastly. She wanted to cover the plasterwork, rip out the fireplace and put a sand-blasted feature wall there instead. Tastes vary, of course,' Gam added, seeing Frances' shocked expression of horror. 'I can't say I liked her very much, but Ian thought she was wonderful. She was strikingly attractive in her way too.

'She was a model and it certainly wasn't a model of behaviour,' Gam added grimly. 'One good thing as far as I was concerned, she soon ripped Ian off! And that finished it, of course. If there wasn't a lot of money she wasn't interested!' Gam laughed. 'It's the first time I've ever been grateful for death duties!' She paused. 'Sometimes I wonder if he will get married now. He goes out a lot, I know, but he's not had any long relationship with a girl since. The old Ian was such a happy lad,' she mused, 'you would have been very happy together.

Now, I'm not sure. I don't want you hurt, my dear.' She looked slowly at Frances. 'I've noticed you don't come over if there's any likelihood of Ian being around, and I've noticed that Ian doesn't visit Jenny if you're likely to be around!' She smiled. 'If it's any help I know he likes to know what you're up to! I think he's trying to reconcile all the work you do and the way you look after the boys with the fact that you're very beautiful and do modelling. For some reason he's given you the same character as his old flame! Now I've said my little piece, so let's have a brandy. I think we could do with one!'

Gam poured two good measures into the lovely old glassware. It was very quiet sitting in the sunshine in the lovely old room. Some of the peace of the room assuaged the hurt in Frances' heart. She was glad Gam had told her; it made it so much easier to understand Ian's behaviour. She knew Gam was warning her, yet at the same time there had been a plea for compassion. She gulped down the fiery liquid and it stung its way into her body.

'Now, Frances, I'll show you upstairs another day. Why don't you have a wander in the trees? I find them very restful.'

Affectionately, Frances hugged Gam. 'Thanks, Gam.' She knew that there had been enough talk, now she wanted to think. Idly she walked across the sweeping lawn and into the band of trees. Gradually she let their beauty seep into her being, even the trees seeming to draw her gently to ease. She hardly noticed their variety and grandeur as she thought over what Gam had said. Although she knew why Ian had behaved as though she was so cheap morally, it didn't lessen her desire to keep out of his way. She wished she had met him before he had become so embittered over her sex. Unfortunately he was so good-looking and with his sheer physical attraction girls would be easy prey, thus reconfirming his opinions. Frances squirmed inside herself as she recalled her abandoned pose in the moonlight. She knew a pang of shame that she had reacted so immediately to his touch and remembered his searing words, 'As it happens it's a bit too blatant for my taste, get some other guy to oblige.' The memory of the words hurt just as badly as before and tears trickled slowly down her face. Finally she pulled herself together. She had work to do and so long as Ian stayed away she could cope. She called goodbye to Gam, who looked sympathetically at the proud young figure. Frances drove down the tree tunnel and back to the farm, her heart sore.

Mechanically she helped Jenny with tea, and afterwards she played with the boys until they went to bed. She felt restless so decided on a swim. One thing—she had no fear of Ian appearing now for a late swim. She swam several lengths, then let herself float in the water. Even her swimming let down her sore spirit and she hauled herself wearily from the water and went to bed, where she lay awake wondering how she could continue to be lighthearted in front of Jenny and the boys.

As it happened it proved easier than she had imagined. The next day was a clinic day, so they left early, wanting to avoid the heat. The three boys wanted to do some of their Christmas shopping. They had hacked open their moneyboxes that morning and their father had given them some extra money for 'wages'. Happily they put on their town wear and Frances and Jenny were affected by their high spirits, and the trip in to the clinic passed in a flash. This time Jenny dropped them at McKenzies, driving herself the short distance to the doctor's. The boys had many anxious huddles discussing a variety of possible purchases. Thad wanted to go to Minsons, a specialist china and glass shop nearby. Apparently he knew exactly what he wanted, for he came out clutching a long slender parcel. 'It's fragile, would you mind carrying it, please?' His brown eyes sparkled. 'It's for Mum.' Gingerly Frances took it, placing it carefully in her shopping bag. Then they crossed to a department store where Ivan bought some shoelaces for his beloved Uncle Ian. 'He broke one yesterday and he had to use string on his workboots!' Thad had a moment of agony when the Scout knife he wanted to buy for himself proved too expensive. Regretfully he replaced it and turned to the toy section. Seeing he was busy there, Frances suggested it to Ivan and Greg, who seized the idea with great alacrity. They bought it while Frances wandered back to Thad to keep his attention diverted. She was rewarded with a big wink from Ivan when they returned, the parcel clutched in Greg's hand. It went into the bag too.

Frances was sorry Rupe and Jenny were not there, it was such a fun-filled time. They visited a toy shop and from there went to meet their mother. She had promised to buy them Kentucky fried chicken for their lunch and they were looking forward to this treat. They found her waiting for them, the red and white striped boxes containing chicken and chips piled beside her. It took a few minutes to drive out to Deans Bush, where they made a picnic for themselves. After the meal Jenny and Frances rested comfortably while the boys ran up and down the paths, playing scant attention to the unique flora around them.

Frances asked how Jenny had got on at the clinic and was pleased that everything was normal. 'He says it's the best I've ever been, and that's a large part thanks to you. I do feel so much easier too. Not long to go now, just under a month.'

The hour passed quickly, then the boys returned wanting to know if they could finish their shopping. They decided to complete it at Riccarton, the big mall being very convenient. Frances slipped away to ring home, but was disappointed as her mother and Kathy were out. Perhaps they were shopping for Christmas too. It took quite a while for the boys to be satisfied with their purchases, and they were tired when they returned to the farm. Jenny made some soup while they unloaded the car, then the boys went to bed as soon as they had finished their meal. Jenny looked tired, but she assured Frances that she would be right after a good night's sleep.

Frances watched television for a while, but she felt too full of restlessness to sit still. She decided to go for a run and went into her bedroom to put on her jeans and top. She checked with Jenny, who grimaced cheerfully and said she was welcome! The men were still out, but she knew by the nightfall that Rupe would be home shortly. During the harvesting the men were busy from daylight to dusk.

Frances hadn't seen Ian for some time now and as she ran she could admit to herself that was probably a good thing. She only had to think of him for the ache inside her to become a throbbing pain. Resolutely she concentrated on running, her pounding feet driving out her thoughts. The night air was soft and still, not as warm as she had expected. She enjoyed her run and decided to go down to the river, the coolness of the night a sharp change after the heat of the day. She slackened her pace to a steady rhythmic gait, leapt lightly over the gate and continued towards the river. The moonlight flickered with clouds at times, but she was so intent she didn't notice. The scene of the river in the moonlight was one to delight the senses. The air was full of the tang of the soft grasses and the scent of lupins. The bands of the river glinted blackly, here and there a glimmer of silver, among the grey stones.

To the west lay the foothills leading up to the giant Southern Alps. Tonight the mountains seemed stark and unreal, like cardboard cutouts on a stage. On the tops traces of snow shone whitely in the soft radiance of the moon. Frances leaned against a willow enjoying the silver display. Above, the stars shone brightly. She picked out the Southern Cross, then Sirius the bright, and found Orion's belt and sword. Then the scene blackened as clouds drifted over the moon again. She shivered, realising with a start how long she had been. She studied the land behind her and knew she could cut a sizeable distance by taking a short cut across Ian's land. It was nearly eleven, so she knew he would be in bed. In town she would have been up, most likely, but here in the country the early dawn meant going early to bed.

She set off quite happily, if slightly chilled by the cold air, glancing around and realising that a bank of clouds had driven up. It looked as though it would rain soon. She increased her speed easily and jogged across the stubble of the recently cut hay paddocks. She climbed carefully over the fence into Ian's farm, her path a wide angle. She was now very close to Coppers and already some of its trees shielded her. The house was in darkness, though, she was relieved to see. She had one more gate to climb and she would be back on Rupe and Jenny's farm. Breathing a sigh of relief because she hadn't enjoyed the feeling of being on Ian's property, she sped up and putting out a hand vaulted over the gate—at least, that had been her intention. The trees had inked out the gate and she had tripped heavily, crashing on to the hard ground with a bone-shaking shock.

She lay there numbly for a few seconds, getting her breath again as pain ripped at her legs. Gingerly she examined herself. Her hands were slightly scratched, but she rubbed them casually against her shirt, bending to see her leg. A dark stain was seeping through her slacks and she eased herself forward to roll up her cuff. As she did so her other leg moved and she writhed in agony at the sharp stab in her ankle. She pulled off her shoe, watching wryly as her ankle swelled. She pulled her lacy handkerchief from her pocket, wishing she had something sturdier to help stop the blood pouring from her other leg. At last the bleeding slowed and finally stopped as she applied pressure. Frances doubted if she could walk far, but decided that after a few moments rest she would try. No one would miss her till morning, she knew. If only it was a warm night she probably would have been uncomfortable but unharmed by a night out. As it was, she was cold and the rain would bucket down soon. The wind now was not the hot, soft gentle nor-wester but a sharp stinging southerly.

She pulled herself up, forcing back the waves of pain by clinging to the gate beside her. When she finally managed it she stood triumphantly, but her left foot could not be put to the ground. 'Well,' she muttered, 'I can't go on standing like a one-legged stork all night.' Hopping on one leg, she reached the gatepost, clinging desperately as beads of sweat broke over her. Her good leg had started bleeding again and she went through her pockets until she found another handkerchief, but the blood kept on spurting through her fingers. She felt dizzy but clung on to the fence, determined to get home. Forcing herself to concentrate on stopping the bleeding, she removed her other shoe and used her sock in an attempt to mop up. Finally the pressure worked and she again attempted to hop along.

Behind her, Coppers was hidden by the trees as she struggled along the fence. She wondered if she should call for help, but resolutely pushed the thought away. Ian would only think she was trying some other ploy, she thought. The rain caught her as she left the shelter of the trees, crashing mercilessly around her. She knew she was feeling strange and when she fell to the ground the lassitude in her body seemed to make her want to do nothing but just to lie there. A warning flashed through her that it was dangerous and she struggled up, not surprised her leg was covered in blood. Its warmth felt strange and Frances felt suddenly that she had made the wrong decision. She should have tried to call out or attract attention when she had been so close to Coppers. Again she forced herself to apply pressure on her leg. Reluctantly she removed her shirt and tied it into place. Perhaps if she struggled back to the trees she could find shelter and conserve her energy. She found comfort in telling herself that it was after midnight and Rupe would be up by six. It wasn't long to wait, if only her leg would stop bleeding. She wished Scamp was with her; several times she had taken him on her nocturnal jogging expeditions, but tonight she hadn't thought of it. She whistled, trying to cheer herself up by imagining all sorts of pleasant things. A dog barked somewhere and she realised it was Ian's black huntaway. She carried on whistling as she stood up and seeing her leg had stopped bleeding she kept on hopping. It was a gallant effort, but she crashed again, not sure which way she wanted to go. The rain was blinding her, but it felt kind to let it dribble against her skin, washing away the mud. Half consciously she whistled before she was overtaken by the strange numbness.

It was a strange fantasy to imagine—Ian bending over her and carrying her chilled body. Frances even imagined the feel of his neck as she curved her hands there for support, nestling against his warm body. Then he was gone and she cried because the fantasy had been so real. She struggled against a fiery heat that seemed to cushion her, reaching out for Ian and only relaxing when she felt his touch and heard his voice tell her that it was all right. She tried to tell him it wasn't, that she mustn't go near him because he thought she was a tramp, but it was too mixed up and she was so cold, and her leg was bleeding and wouldn't stop. Then Ian seemed to be there and others as well, and she drifted into a warm haven, holding on to the warmth and comfort of the strong hands.

She came to consciousness gradually from a strange warm cloud that seemed to be on her forehead. She found strength to open her eyes eventually, but the light was bright and she shut them quickly, wanting to rest in that warm cocoon. Gradually she adjusted, memory of her fall washing over her as she realised her legs were strange.

Her eyes opened properly now and she focussed on the room about her. It was darker now and her startled gaze took in the size of the room she was in. It seemed to be enormous, and the ceiling was studded with small cupid figures clutching plaster draperies and flowers. A glance towards the window confirmed her thoughts. The room angled itself into a large bay forming a circle. She knew now. Obviously Ian had found her and now she was lying in his bed. She tried fretfully to remember what had happened. There was a dim memory of his touch and his warmth, but perhaps that had been only a dream. It must have been, she thought idly. He reserved only contempt for females other than his family.

She felt strange, lightheaded almost, and guessed she must have been drugged. Her fingers caught at the unfamiliar nightgown she was wearing and she realised it must have been one of Gam's. It was a pretty Victorian style in a warm voluminous flannelette, pale blue with sprigs of wild roses printed on to it. With its pintucked front the gathers fell softly from the yoke. Gingerly Frances felt her legs. One was heavily bandaged the other was bandaged at her ankle. She tried to get up, but felt far too sleepy to make much effort, so she decided to doze again.

When she woke again she felt as though she was being studied. She lifted her eyes up, then focussed on the tall figure at the side of the bed.

'Hi, water baby! My, what some folks do instead of taking an ordinary shower! Tell me, is rain good for the complexion?' He chatted quietly, not expecting any reply as he felt her forehead in a professional manner. 'Mm—no fever! Right, let's see your gorgeous legs, water baby.' He lifted the blankets back gently and was quiet while he concentrated on changing the dressing. 'It takes a little while, soon be over,' he continued almost as though she was a child. 'Right, you'll probably always have a scar there, but it'll not spoil your legs, so don't fret!' He replaced the blankets and tucked her in firmly.

'Thank you,' said Frances meekly. 'I'm afraid I can't remember getting here.'

'You can thank the dogs. They started kicking up a racket, so I got up to give them a piece of my mind and I thought I heard someone whistle. So I let Blackie off and when he took off like a shot I followed. I must admit you gave me a hell of a fright, water baby!' He paused. 'I brought you back here, Gam called the doctor and we warmed you up.'

Slowly Frances nodded her understanding. 'Thank you. I'm sorry I've been a nuisance. I'll get up and go back to Jenny's now.'

She struggled to sit up and finally managed to swing her legs over the side of the bed. Her legs seemed very strange and she still could not put weight on her ankle despite its strapping. Ian caught her to him as she fell, scooping her back to bed in an angry gesture.

'You'll stay in bed until I say, understand? Otherwise you'll only get sick and delay your recovery. In the meantime you can eat what Gam gives you.' He grinned suddenly. 'Jenny's sent over some of your night gear, so you can change later on if you want to. This garment is hardly revealing. I think I'd rather have you in your own.'

'I like it, thank you!' Frances retorted, her spirits rapidly rising. 'Actually I do feel hungry.'

'Right. I'll tell Gam and she'll probably fix you something.' His hand idly twisted a curl on her pillow in farewell.

After he had gone Frances snuggled into the depths of the bed. She felt quite ridiculously happy, which was silly, of course, but perhaps was a reaction from whatever the doctor had given her. It was only a few minutes before Gam bought her a delicious omelette and tea. Frances sat up, delighted to see her. Gam filled in some more of the blank spaces, while she ate the omelette.

Frances thanked her gratefully and made a special point of asking if she had any more of the delightfully modest nighties. Gam's eyes twinkled and she said she would be able to find another somewhere.

'Ian dumped you here as the warmest place for you once you were cleaned up. It would have taken a couple of hours to air beds in the spare rooms. I could have let you have my bed, but Ian said his was better, as he has the dressing room where he could sleep and watch you.'

Frances digested this information slowly, her eyes going to the dressing room she guessed was through the door. The thought of Ian nursing her was oddly mixed, and she cuddled into the big folds of the bed for reassurance. Gam gave her a tablet the doctor had left for her and she swallowed it obediently. Then Gam took the tray and she settled to sleep.

It was night when she woke and she whimpered, frightened by the darkness, thinking she was still in the sodden darkness of the field. Even as she struggled to sit up Ian was there holding her gently, soothing her quietly. Contented again, Frances held on to his hand and settled again.

The morning came and she felt lousy, dry-tongued, scratchy and with a headache. She gladly drank the orange juice Ian bought her. She sipped it slowly and he walked out to get some dressings. Quickly she put down the glass and swung her legs to the side. This time she must get up. However, she held the edge of the bed for support and had to bite back a cry from the pain. She staggered when she saw Ian walking in and flung herself anxiously back onto the bed.

'I'll do your leg again,' he said shortly. Frances let him minister to her, appreciating the deftness and delicacy of his touch. When he finished that he put ice on her ankle, then restrapped it after a few minutes. To her comment he said simply that he had taken a course in it some time ago.

'Ian, I'm sorry I panicked last night.'

'That's O.K., water baby. I half expected it. That's why I slept in there. Gam wanted to, but I wouldn't let her. She's some gal, but she's been on the road too long to have to start having broken sleep. Besides, I'm not busy at the moment, it's been raining so hard all harvesting has stopped for a while.'

Despite his words Frances didn't see him for the rest of the day. Gam came up and chatted to her and Jenny and the boys rang up. It made her feel slightly ridiculous at the bother she had caused. In the evening Ian redressed her leg and carried her to the bathroom again. She was pink with embarrassment as he waited by the door for her to complete her ablutions. When she was ready he picked her up and placed her gently in the bed again. In the meantime he had remade it, and Frances curled up gratefully.

He disappeared for a while, then returned with her dinner on a tray. After she had eaten he removed the tray and returned with a cassette recorder and a stack of tapes. He plugged it into the electric plug by the bed and showed her how to operate it, placing it on the bed beside her. The music flooded the room with a tremendous volume of sound and they both reached for the switch instinctively.

'Must have turned it up the last time I used it,' Ian laughed. He adjusted it so that the music could be listened to, yet was not too obtrusive. Frances was glad to have the music. It gave her something safe to talk about and judging by the variety of the tapes, Ian's taste in music was catholic. He sat on the chair by the window, half looking at her or out the window, and she found great enjoyment in discussing the music. She noticed his foot tapping in time to the beat and smiled at the involuntary movement. Together they listened to a recording of a well known pianist's rendition of a Chopin study and the quiet elegance of the music wrapped itself around them. When it was over Frances sighed deeply and Ian switched off and unplugged the recorder.

'I'll leave it here and you can use it tomorrow morning. I'll pick you up at lunchtime and take you downstairs if you feel up to it.'

He looked at her as he said 'Goodnight', then he went to his dressing room, and she determinedly shut her eyes. Later she heard him showering, and a smile lit her face as she heard him burbling away. His voice was rich and powerful, his chest producing a resonant bass. The music was not familiar to her and she wondered if it was from a modern opera. She settled into bed, oddly content with the thought of Ian's closeness.

The morning sun played upon her face and woke her with its warm fingers. After the greyness of the sky it seemed a token of her mood. She limped out of bed to the bathroom and dressed herself slowly. After breakfast Ian reappeared and dressed her legs, doing so apparently with complete ease.

'That's better.' He studied her and a smile flashed in his face. 'Looks like I've lost my Modigliani this morning—yesterday you were all grey blue and sharp angles!'

'Thanks for nothing!' retorted Frances.

'I'll put you over here in the window seat. You've probably had enough of bed.' He bent down and lifted her easily, putting her into the winged chair in the centre of the room. For an instant the physical contact flashed between them, broken naturally by Frances' exclamation of the view.

The trees surrounded and protected the lawn, a strip of them curling to form the drive to the road. Past them the paddocks lay spread out in a neat geometric design of green and gold, laced with the darker threads of fencing and splotched with the black of the trees. In the distance the river shimmered and sparkled in the sunshine. From downstairs there had been no inkling of the spectacular view from Ian's room. Evidently the additional height gave so much more beauty over the tops of the trees.

'It's beautiful,' Frances said simply.

'I think so.' Ian smiled at her and the intimacy of that moment lingered as something almost palpable between them.

'Like true beauty, the more you study, the more it reveals,' Ian said quietly. His glance studied her as though he was asking what she could reveal. Then he turned and was gone, and she was left feeling strangely bereft. She looked back to the windows and gratefully felt the sunshine on her face. There were more clouds massing, but at the moment she was content to sit and dream. She wondered how many times Ian had sat here looking over this land letting his mind soak in the beauty. Circumstance had forced her entry into his most private citadel and the glimpses of the real Ian were tantalising. It seemed strange that the man who had been so cruel and scornful to her now showed a rare gentleness and sensitivity. Frances wondered if he would change once she was well and returned to work for Jenny and Rupe.

Gam came up shortly afterwards bearing coffee and hot scones. 'Ian said you were looking better, and he was right.' She poured Frances a cup of coffee.

'I'm sorry I'm putting you to so much trouble, Gam.'

Gam twinkled, 'Yes, it is a trouble—and a good thing too! Have a scone, Frances, you're overdue for fattening up. A puff of wind would weigh more, I think.'

The scones were delicious and Frances could feel her strength recovering. After morning tea Gam bustled about tidying up and chatting about a variety of topics. She passed Frances her make-up case and perfume and Frances felt more like herself with her make-up on. It couldn't hide the pallor and fragility of her face, but with a soft brush of eye-shadow and a hint of blusher she was able to improve her appearance.

She brushed her hair, spending a lot of time on it. It had managed to pick up a lot of mud, most of which had been brushed out earlier, but it now responded to the brush, to lie softly gleaming around her head.

'I've brought you along one of my native trees and plants books to have a look through. This one in particular has some remarkable paintings, quite exquisitely detailed. I think we can learn such a lot from the world around us. There's a section of the native vines which is particularly absorbing.' She handed Fran a large book, then, seeing its heaviness, she pulled a wine table over so she could read it without having to bear its weight.

Frances wondered what Gam was trying to say, but gave it up and turned to the book. It was easy to become absorbed, but after Gam had left very quiet. She switched on the tape recorder and popped a cassette into its obliging jaw, enjoying the sound which flooded the room. Vaguely Frances studied the section Gam had pointed out. She had been under the impression from Gam's comments that she could profit by learning something by studying the pages on vines. There were many of them, all quite different, some with spectacular flowers, others bearing more insignificant flowers. She closed the book, having convinced herself she would have to ask Gam later what she had meant, then dozed quietly, letting the music roll over her.

CHAPTER SEVEN

IAN's touch on her cheek wakened her and her eyelids fluttered, her eyes enlarging as she looked at him.

'Come on, water baby, put your arms around me and I'll take you downstairs.' His tone was casual and flippant as he bent to pick her up. She curled herself still half sleepily against the warmness of his body reaching out her hands against the back of his neck. His closeness awakened her thoroughly and she stiffened, only to hear Ian say quietly, 'Relax, water baby, I'm not going to drop you.'

Perhaps for a moment she could pretend Ian loved her, that he was holding her because he wanted to. Unwittingly she sighed and curved herself closer to him. It was so good to cling to his strength. Her eyes gleamed as she twigged what Gam had been saying earlier about clinging vines. However, the thought that her action could be interpreted by Ian as a provocation made her stiffen again. They were downstairs now and he put her down in the sunroom in one of the comfortable seagrass chairs. He pulled up another chair opposite so she could rest in a comfortable pose. She was very aware of her heightened heartbeats and hoped Ian had not been conscious of them.

He lifted over a small table and put it beside her as she thanked him.

'I'll claim payment one day,' he grinned, and turned to help Gam carry in a tray with bowls of soup.

Conversation over lunch was easy and Frances was surprised to find how much she enjoyed the meal. Gam was such a lively person and with a fresh audience loved to tell of past history. They hardly noticed the clouds piling up and the gradual darkening of the room until the rain started hitting the windows.

'The washing!' exclaimed Gam, and sped out of the door, followed by Ian. They came back laughing to Frances and dumped the just rescued items on to the cupboard top. Iam helped Gam to fold the clothes, his action completely natural.

'Well, this rain will delay harvesting again, blast it!' he commented ruefully.

'Never mind, you can entertain Frances,' put in Gam. 'I've got a bucket of plums I picked this morning and they must be made into jam this afternoon, so I'll be busy in the kitchen.' Gam dropped Frances an enormous wink and despite herself Frances couldn't resist responding, glad that Ian was still looking out the window.

With Gam's disappearance the room became quiet. Ian got his first aid paraphernalia and redressed her leg. Frances bent down to look and a lock of her copper-gold hair rested lightly on Ian's arm. She flicked it away with a swift apology, but he went on with the dressing, saying easily, 'It's all right. It doesn't bother me.'

It mightn't worry him, but it certainly bothered her, thought Frances. Now she was so much stronger she was vividly conscious of his masculinity. Through his shirt she could see the movement of his muscles as he wound the bandage round her leg. In the beginning he had pushed her skirt back so he could work, and now it had slipped even higher. She wriggled, uncomfortable at the amount of thigh she was revealing and reluctant to pull her skirt lest Ian misinterpret her gesture. Finally Ian completed the dressing and she could flick her skirt into position. She dared not look at Ian lest he have that mocking gleam back in his eyes.

To cover herself she commented on a small wall cabinet which was on the wall above her. It was finely carved and she guessed it was another example of the old Scotsman's work. Ian explained the different pattern to her and she listened to him, absorbing the detail.

Seeing her interest, he went off to fetch a box he kept in his study. He came back with it in his arms, and even from across the room Frances could see its detail.

'It looks fantastic! It's like a Maori design, almost,' said Frances.

'That's observant of you! As a matter of fact my granddad told me that the old Scot admired the symmetry and abstract nature of the Maori carvers. This box was his last work and he called it his life box. He kept all his important papers in it. Before he took ship he gave it to my great-grandfather. It's one of my special treasures.'

Ian picked up her hand and and pressed the imprint of the design on her finger. She looked at it carefully, not thinking of anything except the awareness of physical contact with Ian. He was waiting for her comment, though, so she asked him to explain the design. 'Well, it's based on a vee pattern really, the first line refers to the line of hills the old man came from in Scotland, the second line is a smoother and almost curled vee shape and that represents the waves of the sea. The gap after that is much wider and represents the emptiness and desolation he suffered after losing his wife and child, then the next line, almost flat, is the line of the Rakaia, the line behind that in very steep angles represents the mountains.'

Frances nodded, her eyes going immediately to the centre of the pattern. The flat line seemed to sum up the agony of the old Scot. Her finger strayed to the line of the mountains. Was that a stronger line of triumph after the quietness of the line of the river, or was it just imagination? Ian's eyes were on her and it almost seemed as though he knew what she was thinking, there was such a communion between them.

'You're a perceptive lady,' he muttered, taking the box and striding with it back towards his study. He was back in a minute, suggesting he take her for a walk. Surprised, Frances found that she could manage by holding onto Ian's arm. They only walked about the room for a few paces, then Ian lifted her up and deposited her back in the chair. 'You ate too much dinner,' he laughed. 'You're heavier.'

It covered her embarrassment and she made a retort about his lack of strength which was equally absurd. They had fun testing each other's humour in this way and when Gam called out that afternoon tea was ready Frances held out her hand naturally for his help. Quite unnecessarily he scooped her up, doing it neatly so she was forced to cling on to him. They had afternoon tea surrounded by a bubbling cauldron which smelt delicious. Already there was a stack of plum jam glowing on the bench and it would not be too long before another lot was ready. Gam sent them out of the kitchen speedily and once again Ian carried Frances back to the sunroom.

The rain had stopped and although there were a lot of grey clouds around the sunshine was flickering through. Ian put on a record and they listened to it together, both content to be quiet. When it came to the finish Ian saw that Frances looked pale again, so he bowed elaborately and did an impromptu charade of a coachman and horse which left her laughing. She snuggled against him as he climbed the stairs, his voice saying softly, 'The daring cavalier whisks the lady of his choice to the boudoir.' She joined in with mock sighs and lamentations, then nuzzled her mouth against his throat with an abandoned sigh.

'Forward young hussy,' he whispered in her ear, his voice sending deep ripples of feeling down her body.

Suddenly it was not funny any more and they looked at each other as if they could see the true feeling reflected there. Ian put her on the bed quietly and gently, then stooped to pull out her suitcase. He selected a white nightgown and threw it on to the bed, his foot pushing the suitcase back under the bed.

'Here, you can change O.K.? I'll come back in ten

minutes and give your leg the treatment.'

Frances nodded quietly, relieved to be back on an even keel with Ian. When the door had closed behind him she glanced ruefully at what he had put on the bed. It was a white silk nightgown cut Grecian style with a tie on one shoulder, leaving the other bare. An embroidery of gold thread cunningly wove itself into a key pattern and followed the shoulder line from the tie around the neckline and under the breasts. The silk fell dramatically from there until it reached her feet where the gold embroidery resumed its chase. It was a beautiful garment, but definitely not one she wanted to wear in front of Ian.

She wondered if she could pull another out and tried to reach the bag. However, it was quite impossible, so she looked around for a substitute and was relieved to see her dressing gown hanging on the back of the door. At least she could put that on and be respectable. She changed quickly, lightly creaming her face and rubbing in some perfume behind her ears. She brushed her hair into a mass of curls and slipped the silk over her body. A glance in the mirror reconfirmed her fears. She did look pretty, and the gown was ridiculously revealing, hinting as it did at the curves of her body. She flung the brush down and began to inch her way towards the door and the dressing gown. It was such a vast room, she thought crossly as she moved from bed to table to wall. If she stuck to the wall she would have support, but it would be twice as long. She decided to risk cutting across. Halfway there the door opened and Ian walked in. His hands were full of disinfectant, towel, and gauze strips, but he stood and eyed her appreciately. She froze, not wanting to move, aware that she looked like a statue but unwilling to reveal herself more by movement. Ian laughed. 'You look beautiful, Frances, very desirable.'

He passed her and she heard him put the bandages down on the table. However, he made no attempt to help her, so she steeled herself to walk the remaining few steps and thankfully grabbed her dressing gown. She felt it slip, then it caught in the sleeve and she could have wept with rage at her predicament, knowing the wretched creature behind her was thoroughly enjoying himself.

She leant against the door and turned to face him. 'My gown, please, Ian.'

'I think not, my Greek princess,' he spoke quietly and his eyes caressed her. 'It would go against all my artistic principles to cover that sight.'

Anger flashed from Frances and she tugged again at the gown. If she could put weight on one foot and jump at it she knew it would probably slip off. Tantalisingly it swung above her; obviously the hook had been made for a tall man originally. She pulled at it and behind her heard Ian's dry laugh. It taunted her to action and she jumped on her good foot, reaching the gown, only to collapse as her weak ankle took the unaccustomed weight and she staggered, crying with pain.

Ian picked her up. 'I'm sorry, Frances—I'm a brute.' He kissed her gently. 'You just looked so much a woman I couldn't resist. I forgot myself.' He put her down on the bed. 'I'll get you a drink.'

It seemed only a minute or two before he was back and holding her gently, encouraging her to sip the fiery liquid. He soothed her, holding her slim form against himself. When she was recovered he turned his attentions to her leg, carefully examining her ankle first. He seemed relieved that it was not damaged by her fall, but he strapped it again quite firmly. Her bad leg was painful. He bathed it in disinfectant that stung so dreadfully big tears formed in her eyes and rolled silently down her cheeks. The soothing ointment he put on helped considerably as he applied it carefully. He had looked up and seen the tears, but had not commented until he was ready to wrap it up again. 'Worst is over, water baby.' He pinned it into place, then lifted the blankets carefully over her, tucking in the side.

Frances was glad to rest. She felt weak and her leg still hurt and her ankle throbbed. Dimly she heard Ian clean up the basin and replace the bandages on the cabinet. She mopped her face, glad to be alone. She heard Ian close the door and shortly afterwards heard the roar of his motorbike. Afterwards she had a light tea, only forcing herself to eat to avoid hurting Gam.

Lying in bed, she could see the reflection of the sunset colour the room. The small figures on the ceiling seemed to be washed in pink and gold. There was a deep quiet over Coppers. Frances moved in the big bed. Suddenly it struck her that now she was quite well enough to return to Jenny and Rupe. At least she wouldn't have such a humiliating episode happen again as she recalled the look on Ian's face. She knew she would ask to go home the next day. Strangely the thought did not please her greatly and she sighed restlessly. Why couldn't she make up her mind? she thought.

When she woke it was dark, but a light was burning in the dressing room. It was just after twelve, so obviously Ian could not sleep. She stirred restlessly, trying to find a comfortable spot for her ankle. Her eyes opened to see Ian standing there.

'Nightmare?' he queried, sitting easily and naturally on the bed.

'No. Just woke up, I guess. My ankle is playing up a bit.'

'I'll restrap it for you.' He lifted the bedclothes and eased the bandage off, doing it carefully. The small light in the dressing room behind him silhouetted his figure so the shadow seemed giant size, overwhelming her.

He sat beside her again as he rolled the crêpe bandage slowly while she wriggled her foot. His physical presence was so overpowering that she had difficulty in keeping her breathing steady. Absurdly conscious of her appearance in the wretched nightgown, she could only admire Ian's self-control as he calmly restrapped her ankle and replaced the blankets.

'I'll get you a mug of cocoa and get one of the pills the doctor left for you,' he said evenly. It was not long before he was back handing her the warm drink. Frances was reluctant to take the pills but with Ian's gaze on her she swallowed it obediently. She finished the cocoa and snuggled down into the big bed.

'Couldn't you sleep either?' she asked, her eyes moving over his face.

'No!' He grinned. 'Make the most of that bed, water baby, I'm afraid my legs don't react very well to the one in the dressing room.'

'Never mind. I'll be gone tomorrow, so if you can put up with that bed tonight you can sleep tomorrow. This is a lovely big bed.' She smiled sleepily, her eyes struggling to keep open.

His hand gently brushed the curls from her face. 'Don't be in a hurry to go, water baby. Gam likes having you here.'

He turned and walked back to his dressing room. Frances suddenly felt near to tears. He had not asked her to stay for his own sake but for Gam's. She struggled to remember what he had said. It had been a joke, but perhaps it was the truth disguised. He didn't want her; even though he had been so kind and gentle while she was sick, it would be the same for anyone. A big sob wrenched from her and she muffled the sound in the pillow. 'Oh, why did I have to fall in love with Ian?' she thought glumly. Why should he affect her so powerfully, when she meant nothing to him? In fact he despised her as a woman. She sobbed again. If only she hadn't seen this other side, loving and gentle and funfilled. It had been so wonderful play-acting with him this afternoon, and when he carried her downstairs her heart had raced. She sobbed again and the tears came in earnest.

'Frances, what is it? It's O.K.' Ian's voice in her ear, his arms round her, were some fantasy her mind had dredged up. She sobbed against him as though her heart would break, in an agony of loss. Eventually the storm passed and she was still held safely until she slept dreamlessly.

It was late when she woke in the morning and the house was quiet. She touched her head; it felt woolly and her tongue felt dry and horrid. She edged over to the side of the bed and gingerly put her foot to the ground. To her relief she could walk on it, and she hobbled carefully to the bathroom. She had a shower and dressed, then fixed her leg. The end result was quite neat, but not the professional neatness that Ian had shown. Thinking of him sent stabbing thoughts through her, a recollection of loss, and she sighed deeply. Ian didn't want her here, so she must leave today.

Getting downstairs was an effort and she sat down on the bottom step to recover herself, before she saw Gam. After a few minutes she braced herself to pretend that she felt wonderful and walked into the kitchen with a gay, 'Good morning, Gam.'

'Good morning, Frances. How are you, my dear? Ian told me not to disturb you. He said you had a bad night.' Gam eyed her anxiously.

'Oh, nonsense, Gam,' she said brightly. 'I did wake up, but Ian was very good. He brought me some cocoa and one of those pills to help me sleep, so I was out like a light very quickly.'

'Well, sit down, Frances, and I'll get you some breakfast.'

Gam finished putting away the gleaming golden jars of plum jam and then put the kettle on. Frances made herself some toast. She didn't want to eat at all, but unless she did Gam would be suspicious. As she ate Frances told Gam that she was well enough to return to Jenny and Rupe.

'I'll need help going over there, I'm afraid. It's a bit far to walk and of course the wee Mini is over there. Would you mind taking me later on?'

'Certainly! I'm not too sure you're fit enough, but if you insist, I'll let you go.'

'Thanks, Gam! Every day my ankle is improving so much more. My only worry is driving into town before Christmas.'

'Don't worry! Someone is bound to be going into town. Perhaps after Christmas your parents could bring you back. That reminds me—what about inviting your parents to Coppers one day in the New Year? You told me your father was a barbecue king. Perhaps we could have a barbecue at the river and Ian could take them jet boating at the same time.'

'Oh, Gam! What a lovely idea!' exclaimed Frances, giving Gam a quick hug.

'Now let me look at my diary and I'll give a definite date. I do hate vague invitations. What about the Saturday the sixth or Sunday the seventh? Ring your mother and ask her and perhaps in a day or two you could let me know her answer.'

'Oh, Gam, I know she'd love to come. I'm sure it will be yes.'

After breakfast Frances washed her few dishes and cleared away the food, leaving the kitchen tidy. Then she rang home and was delighted to find her mother and Kathy in. As she had guessed her mother thought it was a lovely idea. Frances passed the phone over to Gam and smiled at the way everything was arranged. Kathy was thrilled to have an invitation to see the farm and her joy came bouncing over the wires. Her mother was concerned to know how she felt, and Frances felt oddly touched to know that Ian had rung her family three times.

Frances climbed upstairs again to pack her bag. She stripped the bed, struggling with the size of it. It was a strange sensation to make it up again knowing that Ian would lie here tonight. She sat down on the bedroom chair to rest and restrap her ankle before she began dusting and polishing.

It was lunchtime as she finished screwing the lid on the polish. She gave the last cabinet a friendly flick, satisfied with her efforts. The whole room smelt deliciously of her perfume and polish. She opened the windows further and saw Ian striding towards the house. Just to look at his tall figure was a delight. He glanced up and catching sight of her, waved. Frances smiled without realising, then turned away to pick up her suitcase. She was halfway down the stairs with it when Ian saw her predicament and ran lightly to take the case from her.

They had lunch together and Frances tried hard to be witty and lighthearted. After lunch Ian said he would help Gam with the dishes while she had a rest for ten minutes. She laid down on the big couch in the lounge, glad to put her feet up again. It seemed only a few minutes before Ian came in with his first aid equipment.

'Oh no! The instrument of torture,' she said lightly to cover her confusion.

'Come on, water baby. It's not that bad, is it?' he smiled. His smile sent her heart beating rapidly and she turned her head away lest he see the look on her face. Again he dressed her leg expertly and it was not so painful today. Even so she was rather white-faced when he finished and he poured her a drink of brandy. He sat beside her, lifting her against himself. His arm was round her to give her extra support and she leaned against him gratefully while she had the drink. It's a little memory, she thought to herself. Once I leave he'll probably only see me as a tramp again. She sighed softly and closed her eyes, enjoying the sweet feeling of content seeping through her. She became aware that Ian's dark eyes were on her face and she felt compelled to look at him, to study his expression. It was a long moment, before he bent his head and kissed her gently and sweetly. Then he took the glass from her shaken fingers and strode away with it into the kitchen.

Frances stood up as he returned and offered her his

arm. He helped her to the car and she climbed in.

''Bye, water baby! See you around.' Gam came out and took the driver's seat. Too late Frances realised she hadn't thanked Ian. She tried to explain to Gam, but she brushed it aside, with a casual word. I'll write to him, Frances thought. As they came out of the tunnel of trees she felt more miserable than ever.

When they arrived Jenny came out to meet them, hugging Frances gently, and the boys' questions tumbled over like rapids as they wanted to know all the details.

'Trust Uncle Ian,' said Ivan, his grin stretching across his face. He was delighted, obviously, to find his favourite uncle very much the hero.

After Gam left with Frances' grateful thanks the rest of the day passed quietly. Frances spent most of the time helping the boys to restring an old hammock they had unearthed. The day had been blustery hot, so she was not surprised to hear that the men would start harvesting again the next afternoon. In the evening Frances rang Coppers to speak to Ian so she could thank him for his efforts, and felt ridiculously hurt when Gam told her that Ian had gone to town. The thought of Ian with some unknown girl caused her considerable pain. She pushed the thought away, then determined to write the thank-you letter. The words in her heart she could not put on paper and it was some time before she drafted a formal note which sounded very stilted. To try to achieve some balance she did a thumbnail sketch of herself in Ian's big bed. After she had sent the boys to deliver it the next day she wondered if that had been the wisest drawing to send. She hoped he would not misinterpret the drawing. At the time its double implication hadn't occurred to her and she hoped Ian wouldn't see it in that light. Thinking of Ian made her realise that he would be highly amused by it and she felt chagrin at her own efforts.

To Rupe's delight the blustery hot wind continued, so

Frances knew the men would be busy again in the afternoon. Jenny and she picked blackcurrants. The fruit hung in small shiny clusters from the twiggy bushes, and they could pick the fruit easily as they sat on the ground. The boys chattered around them like a nest of squawking starlings, alternately squabbling and laughing. Their efforts were added to the pile, but after the second carton of carefully top-'n'-tailed berries was spilt Jenny suggested they get their horses and go for a ride to a young neighbour's place. They whooped with delight; their ideas of pleasure did not include the painstaking patience needed to deal with the juicy fruit. They cleaned themselves up reluctantly, then ran off in great glee. While Frances carried on with the blackcurrants, Jenny picked some raspberries. In the peace of the afternoon they preserved the blackcurrants, reserving some for fruit syrup for winter drinks. Both Jenny and Frances were highly pleased with the day's activities as they surveyed the gleaming jars.

Work on the farm went on, in a steady pattern. Rupe seemed to be perpetually busy and Frances was glad her leg had recovered enough to let her go about her work. Her ankle had gone down to its normal size the day after she arrived home, but she was careful not to push it too hard. Time in the sunshine soon put colour in her cheeks, so apart from a small bandage covering the stitches she was almost back to normal. The stitches caused her only a little discomfort and she was looking forward to having them removed. The doctor had agreed to giving her an appointment on Christmas Eve on her way back to town.

On Christmas Eve Ian came over to take her into town. Originally the plan had been for her to go in with Gam, but in the morning Gam had rung to say Ian would be the driver.

'My dear, my wrist is paining me quite dreadfully. Just occasionally I get this arthritic twinge, so I asked Ian to take you.'

When Frances told Jenny what had happened Jenny looked rather thoughtful.

'Gam's rather a rogue at times. I know she's never had arthritis in her life!' Jenny eyes Frances speculatively. 'If it's what I think, then I hope Gam's plan works! I'm glad you and Gam get on so well together.'

Frances had sent her presents to the family over to Coppers earlier. She was sorry she would not be with them on Christmas, but was looking forward to going home for a week. Her bag was ready and she had dressed in her flouncy skirt with the pintucked shirt. Ian looked at her appreciatively, but said little as he escorted her to the car. She was very conscious of his physical size as she sat oddly meek beside him in the car. He escorted her into the doctor's surgery, waited patiently for her and lent his arm as they went back to the car. He mentioned that he still had a few items to get in town and asked if she wanted to go straight home. Frances felt very formal explaining that her parents knew she would not be home till it was convenient on the farm.

They were lucky enough to get a car-park along by Noah's Hotel. Ian told her how long he would be and Frances settled happily to watch the festive scene. For once the crowd seemed infected with gaiety; strangers greeted others with a smile or a 'Merry Christmas'. The shop lights twinkled out their messages, lighting the floral baskets that hung from the shop verandahs. Even in the twilight fast fading, Frances could see the petunias, fuchsias and trailing ferns in the pretty baskets. The flowers were repeated in the more formal banks of colour in the gardens between the footpath and the river beside her.

Frances decided to mingle with the crowd, and slipped her coat over her shoulders. She studied the shops and the thought came to her to buy Ian a present. She had given Gam and all the others one, but now she felt she must not leave Ian out. A silversmith had his shop not far away, so she walked to it quickly, wondering what Ian would like. An idea came for a medallion of St Christopher. The legend had long been one of her favourites and as Ian had rescued her it seemed appropriate. To her delight the shop had exactly what she wanted, and she felt quite pleased as she made her way to the car.

Close at hand on the riverbank the carollers were striking up. Passersby stopped to join in, adding to the formal choir, while others held candles aloft in the night air. Frances realised then that this was the 'Carols by Candlelight' ceremony and she joined in the group singing. Someone gave her a candle and someone else lit it for her. She kept a watchful eye on the car for Ian's return. When he did come back he glanced around and on seeing her wave crossed to join in. It was quite dark under the willow trees and the glow of the candles flickered above the water of the river. Frances remembered the disastrous night she had spent after looking at the giant rakaia and she shivered. Ian pulled her against him and she stood in the crook of his arm as they sang the old favourites. Overhead the stars shone brightly and the joyful atmosphere of Christmas seemed to spread its peace over all. When the last note of 'Silent Night' had died away they walked quietly back to the car.

Frances gave Ian directions to her parents' home. On their arrival he took her suitcase and escorted her up the drive. Kathy must have heard the car and she came running out to meet them. Ian was introduced to the family and urged to stay for drinks. To Frances' surprise he showed no desire to rush off, but later this was explained by his statement that he intended going to the Cathedral for the midnight service.

Frances went to help her mother, but she came out then with pizzas and savouries piping hot. Kathy seemed to have taken greatly to Ian and as she was almost completely uninhibited questioned him ruthlessly about his farm and his interests. Frances had the greatest difficulty in keeping a straight face over some of Ian's answers. The tactics of children were not wasted on him. Martin arrived with his current girl-friend and more introductions were made. The lights of the tall pine tree flickered on and off as a pattern and around the base of the tree were a number of presents already. When it was time to go to church it seemed natural for Frances to go in Ian's car. Kathy piled in too and they met up with the rest of the family at the stone building, floodlit for the occasion. The choir was already singing carols and the church was packed with people. Frances was conscious of Ian's closeness as they joined in the worship, and when he looked down at her and smiled softly her heart sang. Poor Kathy was very sleepy and rejoined her parents after the service, so Ian and Frances went home alone. Ian drove easily through the sleeping streets. The street lights formed a pattern of shadow and light until he pulled up alongside the river. He turned to Frances and smiled. 'Happy Christmas!' he said, and kissed her gently.

'Happy Christmas!' said Frances, and kissed him just as briefly back.

Shyly she produced her gift. 'It's a thank you, Ian, for rescuing me and for your kindness when I was sick.' Her heart was dancing in her chest as she held out her small gift.

Ian seemed very touched by her gesture. He opened the box and admired the silver disc.

'I'll put it on. It's special because you gave it to me.' He removed his jacket and tie and undid his shirt top buttons. He fumbled the small catch, so Frances took it from him and fastened it round the brown neck. The silver glinted in the faint light against the polished mahogany of his chest.

'I know one way to say thank you,' Ian suggested, drawing her to him. The kiss was a long deep one, sending her response of love crashing against him like waves against rocks. Her heart was unguarded and she knew a deep thrilling joy as she pressed closer to Ian. For a brief moment she felt sure that his response meant he shared her feeling too. It was a shock that left her gasping to feel Ian push her back into the seat and hear the roar of the car's motor. When they arrived home a minute or two later he switched off the engine and turned to face her.

'Despite the Christopher I'm no saint, Frances. But there are limits. I know in the past I wanted to have sex with you.' He paused and Frances staring at him noted the look of strain on him.

'I have to apologise to you, Frances. I don't think I'll ever forget that because of my behaviour you felt you couldn't seek help from me. Instead you almost died.' Frances knew there was a quiet steel in his words. She sat staring at him, trying to see his eyes which were in dark shadow, unknowing that her own were wide with appeal. Neither of them made a move until Ian said quietly, 'Once upon a time I used to dream about a girl like you, someone pretty and spirited, who would need me as much as I needed her. Now I find her, and I'm the one who's wrong. In this tale the prince has turned into a frog. For you there has to be a prince. I'm sorry, water baby.' He opened his door and came round and helped her out. His hand held hers as he took her to the side door. It was open and Frances stepped inside quickly, not wanting him to see the tears in her eyes. He turned her round, though, and studied her, then held her to him, kissing her wet eyelids. 'Your tears are like diamonds in the starlight. Goodbye, Frances.'

She watched him from the hall as he strode quickly down the path. A few seconds later she heard the engine start and then the car moved down the street. Frances tiptoed past her parents' room. In bed at last she felt numbed, but no tears came. She wept inside for Ian, and for the two of them and their love.

Kathy brought her breakfast in bed. She had no desire for food, but she couldn't hurt Kathy by turning down the breakfast she had cooked. Afterwards she showered and put on her prettiest dress of jade satin cotton. With her make-up and her hair swept up into the waterfall style, she was confident she could hide her feelings. She helped her mother and sister with the meal preparations, recounting incidents of life on the farm. Her stay at Coppers was explained and she was able to demonstrate convincingly that her ankle was better. The gash on the other leg she had dressed again that morning, but now all she needed was a light gauze pad on top. Mrs Elaman wisely refrained from commenting about Ian, but Kathy as usual came out with it forthrightly.

'Hey, Sis, what about you and that gorgeous hunk of masculinity?'

Frances made light of it, saying Ian wasn't her type, but from the look on her sister's face she felt sure Kathy didn't agree. Quickly she changed the subject so that Kathy forgot her earlier interest.

Martin arrived then, with Aunt Fay and Uncle William. They moved into the lounge and had a round of drinks while greeting each other. It was Uncle William who was a horse fanatic and he had taught all the Elaman children to ride. Now he too wanted to hear all about life on the farm. Shortly afterwards another group of cousins arrived and Frances and Martin were kept as busy as the Christmas tree lights. The pile of presents sprawled farther into the room, their bright wrappings and bows hinting of joys to come.

The dinner of traditional turkey and roast lamb was magnificent. The table was laden and the silver and crystal sparkled in the light. The cousins had brought along several bottles of champagne and this added to the merriment. Afterwards the men washed up while the women rested and the children waited fretfully for the grown-ups to hurry up. At last the whole party was gathered ready in the lounge and the youngest one selected a parcel and handed it to the right recipient. Then the youngsters handed the other gifts around and the contents were revealed. Soon bright colourful wrappings festooned their way from one end of the lounge to the other.

Frances was delighted with her gifts, some of her favourite French perfume from her parents, a cookbook from Kathy, and Martin had selected an unusual pottery vase. Her uncle and aunt had given her some exquisite silk material in blues and greens and the cousins had given her a box of chocolates. As well there were parcels from Jenny and 'Rupe which Ian must have put in last night. The boys had picked one of the latest top pop cassettes and Gam, Jenny and Rupe had given her an exquisite petticoat and pantie set.

There was another package and the card said Ian, so she slipped it into her pocket. It burnt a hole against her hand as she sat through afternoon tea and the Christmas cake being cut and eaten. This year Kathy had helped her mother with the cake. It had been one of Frances' special jobs as a youngster and this was the first time she had missed. However, Kathy had been made to feel special. She had kept it simple with white icing peaked to look like snow and a miniature tree made from cutting a few inches from the end of the branches of the cedar tree in the garden. Kathy had dabbed spots of the white icing to look like snow on the tree and highlighted it by sprinkling it with shiny cashews. Frances was most impressed and complimented Kathy sincerely. The neighbours arrived and more chatter and small gifts were exchanged, then despite protestations that they couldn't eat anything a cold buffet was served of salads, ham, cold turkey, surrounded by fruit and Pavlova.

Frances gave her mother a quick glance. As usual she was busy looking after others, but there was no sign of tiredness. Mrs Elaman loved entertaining and cooking was one of her delights. Frances and Martin and Kathy cleaned up afterwards. The rest had drifted back to the lounge and when Martin and Kathy joined them, Frances slipped out into the garden.

CHAPTER EIGHT

FRANCES felt in her pocket for Ian's present and with fingers shaking opened it carefully. Inside lay a small silver brooch with a design of a tree. One branch of the tree sparkled greenly with tiny leaves of jade. The card was plain but neatly printed: 'Keep a green bough in your heart and one day the singing bird will come.' It was an old proverb, but not one Frances knew. The message seemed to bring hope. She looked at the brooch carefully, admiring its delicate charm. It was beautiful and she knew it had been selected with considerable thought. Yet it seemed paradoxical. Ian had turned away from her, yet he had given her this present. Without him how could the singing bird come?

Carefully Frances pinned the brooch on to her dress knowing it would look exquisite against the jade colours. Then reluctantly she faced the family again, slipped in unnoticed except for Martin, whose eyes raised in a slight question. She smiled back at him and, satisfied, he turned back to listen to his uncle. Soon afterwards the fun of Christmas charades began. Frances had prepared hers before, 'Is a bang-up time a Christmas cracker?' and to her delight young Kathy worked it out very quickly.

At last the guests departed and Frances could go to bed. She unpinned the brooch carefully and put it back into its box, with the card. Slightly grimly she wished she could dispose of the ache in her heart so neatly.

Weariness of body and spirit seemed to engulf her as she lay in bed. It had been a memorable Christmas, she thought ruefully. Her leg ached, throbbing painfully, and it was echoed by the pain in her heart. The one thought to cheer her was the message, 'Keep a green bough in your heart and one day the singing bird will come'.

Everyone slept late the next day until Kathy pulled the rest out of bed, declaring they were all turning into Christmas bedbugs. There was a flurry of activity to straighten the family home after the festivities of the day before. During lunch Martin suggested they go to the beach for the afternoon and everyone seemed to agree on this idea. Frances was glad she had slipped in her bikini when packing for the week at home.

It took only fifteen minutes to drive to Sumner Beach. The younger people were ecstatic to see the enormous rollers breaking in white foam to leave lacy frills upon the sand. Mr Elaman decided to drive to the Scarborough end of the beach. It was very rocky, having only a small sandy strip, but because of that it was less crowded.

Mrs Elaman, Kathy and Frances had worn their swimsuits out, so it was not long before they were tip-toeing into the water. Kathy screamed with mock terror when a large wave reached her knees and Mrs Elaman won the race to get wet with a remarkable dive through the following wave. Kathy wasn't going to be beaten by Frances and the two glanced at each other before diving together through the next wave. Martin had disappeared with his surfboard earlier and Mr Elaman joined them in the waves. He had bought a large soccer ball and the whole family had enormous fun leaping and diving after it through the waves. Frances kept thinking about Ian and wondering how he would enjoy the scene. The force of the water surged over her suddenly and she spluttered and coughed, tasting the salt in her mouth. Kathy grinned and said something cheeky to an incoming board rider and it made Frances realise how far they had drifted in the currents. Kathy rejoined her parents on the sand, but Frances struck out through the waves, wanting to release the pent-up feeling of anguish. She should not have been surprised to reach the surfboard riders' playground and one of them, a friend of Martin's, recognised her. He signalled for her to join him on his board and Frances scrambled up willingly. Last year she had spent quite a lot of time in the surf at weekends and if conditions were right, after work too. Now she was faced with picking the wave, and seeing the gleam in her partner's eye and his quick nod she leaned against him as they stood on the tip of the wave. The wave carried them shorewards in crashing splendour, the swift movement demanding instant responses of their bodies. It was a thrill to feel the wind and the wave rushing past, and Frances exultantly turned to her partner, seeing the look of delight echoed in his eyes, before she was crashing through the water. She came up laughing at herself for forgetting the original laws of gravity and waved an apologetic farewell to Martin's young friend before striking out to the shore. She was surprised how much strength it took to make the shore and realised she had been rather stupid in venturing so far. Her mother was pouring hot coffee and she drank the liquid thirstily. Martin rejoined them too and they sat in easy companionship, content to lie in the sun.

About four o'clock Mr Elaman declared that he felt like a barbecue. The rest of the family cheered because he was acknowledged as an expert. It didn't take long to shrug the sand off themselves and return home. Mr Elaman had built his own brick barbecue some years before and over the years had collected some impressive hardware. Martin and Kathy piled wood from the garage ready for the expert's touch. He was happy to explain that he found wood a good base to build up a pile of ash, using only a very little charcoal. The neighbours joined in too and the aroma of wood smoke soon drifted in the evening air. Frances grinned at the sight of her father demonstrating the art of cooking chops, steaks and sausages, pointing out the places to sear and where to cook. She filled a glass of beer for him and stood watching as he expertly turned the meat, being careful not to allow the juices to disappear into the flames. Martin hooked up the loudspeaker and played some of the latest pop tunes. Frances ate a chop; the flavour was deliciously tangy and the side salad and beetroot and cucumber went with it well. She sat on one of the outdoor chairs under the walnut tree, letting its green leaves give her privacy as she watched the party.

Martin was flirting lightly with their neighbour's daughter and Frances could see the pleasure in the young girl's face. She had been a bit of a pest around the place when she was younger, wanting to tag along with Martin, but now she kept her distance and Martin was the one to do the running. Perhaps in a few years both of them would settle to a permanent relationship—who knew? Frances looked at their fun and sighed deeply. She felt about nine hundred years old tonight, lost and desolate. The memory of Ian's gift seemed only to taunt her, for how could she keep a green bough in her heart when she felt so alone? She chided herself for her weak selfishness and began to clear up the stack of paper dishes, burning a number of them on the now almost dead barbecue, sending the flames flaring again. The cutlery she rinsed through before putting it into the dishwasher, then carefully she refrigerated the rest of the food. She felt very weak and her leg throbbed, so she decided to go to bed. Perhaps she had overdone the exercise, she thought ruefully as she changed into her nightclothes. She put on the white Grecian gown, remembering when she had worn it last in a small agony of feeling. It was a joy to recall Ian and the look of his dark eyes and the crinkle of laughter lines on his face. She went over again the words he had said at their last meeting, his apology, and his farewell. It had been so unutterably final; she forced herself to face it now and to acknowledge the searing agony that racked her.

In the morning she got up early and began cleaning out the kitchen cupboards. It took her some hours and the rest of the household appeared and disappeared according to their whims. They appeared to be spending a lot of time in bed, thought Frances; life on the farm had become such a habit that early rising seemed natural. In the afternoon she took Kathy to town to buy a pair of shorts. Kathy had received the money for Christmas and she had made Frances promise her that she would help her find a pair. It took some time to get the right cut and the right colour and they had traipsed through a number of shops before finding exactly what they wanted. Triumph showed in every line at last and they walked back to the car, pleased with the purchase. That night they went to a movie together and afterwards they sat round discussing it. There was an easy camaraderie and Frances knew how lucky she was that her family shared so much joy together.

On New Year's Eve they gathered in their next door neighbour's yard for a barbecue and pool party. Their other neighbours were there too, this being a more or less easy traditional gathering. Some brought hot garlic bread, others coleslaw, others wine and beer, some salads and meat. Frances smiled to see her father happily playing chef; he would have felt quite hurt if that chore had been given to some other hand. It was a happy atmosphere, office and shop routines forgotten with the holidays. Frances was the object of the attentions of two overgrown schoolboys, much to young Kathy's disgust. Despite her lack of interest they scurried round vying for her attention, and even paid Kathy a compliment or two in an attempt to curry favour. Eventually they realised that Frances was not encouraging them and they turned their efforts to swimming. Earlier Frances had decided not to go into the pool. Her leg was healing beautifully, but she didn't want to risk any infection. In the sea she had felt no qualms about it, but in the pool, despite its filtration system, she hesitated. The night stars were bright and she shivered suddenly as a cloud went over the moon. It reminded her of her nightmare experience and she longed for the comfort of Ian's presence. Instinctively she closed her fingers round the tiny silver brooch she had clipped on earlier, her fingers feeling automatically for the tiny leaves of greenstone. The cloud shifted and the moonlight shone again. Somewhere a pop record blared out and one of the young men appeared, asking her to dance. She tried, but found the movement worried her ankle, so she guided her partner to Kathy, who willingly jumped at the chance for a 'proper dance'. At midnight everyone joined in a big circle and sang 'Auld Lang Syne' as the clock struck. There was much kissing and hugging as everyone wished each other a Happy New Year. The party would continue for some time and there was not a chance of sleeping if she went home.

Quietly Frances slipped along the drive and out into the street. She headed towards the river, seeking its quietness and peace. Most of the surrounding houses were quiet now, although here and there a light glowed. Frances felt totally relaxed in these quiet streets. They were familiar and safe, she had jogged along here hundreds of times. She turned a corner and found herself following the course of the river, a mere creek at this stage but made beautiful by the trees beside it. She rested against one of the trees, its trunk forming a backrest. Glancing around, she realised this was the spot where Ian had kissed her on Christmas night. The leaves fluttered briefly above her and the water rippled and sang as it danced its way to the sea. It gleamed black with silver patches glinting suddenly where the street light caught a ripple. It made her smile to remember her last moonlight run to the mighty Rakaia. This she could possibly jump over, but the Rakaia was so wide. Even its name told a lot, for 'Rakaia' referred to the way to ford it, and meant 'where strong men stand in rows'. Strong men of the tribe would stand together holding a line and breaking the force of the current so the women and weaker members could walk in safety. Frances smiled at the comparison of this small river, yet it too could prove treacherous and flooded regularly. As quietly as she had come she stood up and made her way home. It was very early in the morning and the revels had ceased from next door. Faint smells of the giant barbecue still held in the night air and she wrinkled her nose.

She slept later the next morning, then went to church with her family to celebrate. Afterwards they had another fabulous meal and Mrs Elaman was delighted to receive the praise her avocado vinaigrette, followed by crayfish poached in wine, deserved. The household retired early and Frances too slept. Her time at home was almost over and Mr and Mrs Elaman were determined to make the most of the day. They drove together to Spencer Park, a beach reserve not far from Christchurch. They passed the camping ground and swept past the playground surrounded by pine trees. As they were early they had plenty of time to set up a good picnic spot with plenty of shade. Later they were pleased they had that forethought as the day turned out to be a real scorcher, with temperatures high in the thirties. Lying under the trees reminded Frances of Ian and she walked restlessly to the beach. Today the water was warm to her touch and she enjoyed the crashing waves, diving through them in delight. Mr Elaman had insisted they stay within the flagged areas as the beach had many danger spots with channelling and rips. Kathy joined her and shrieked with mirth when a large lump of seaweed wrapped itself round her leg. The next giant wave crashed over them and they surfaced grinning at each other. Martin came in then bringing the beach ball and threw it to land with a loud slap, sending diamond sparkles into the air. Kathy swam after the ball, the waves carrying it rapidly back to shore. She caught up with it, then threw it to Frances, who sent it spinning back to Martin. A wave caught him unexpectedly and he flopped back in an effort to catch it. Kathy found she had to rescue it again and declared it was too rough for such sport.

They spreadeagled themselves in the sun to dry, but the intense heat sent them back through the sandhills to their picnic spot, the sand burning their toes in the jandals. It was quite dark when they returned home many swims later and Frances was able to sleep from exertion and the healthy sea air.

The next day she packed her bag and put it ready in the sunroom. Jenny was due at the gynaecologist's clinic and Gam would drive her in. Frances had told her mother that they would pick her up and Kathy spent most of the day running towards the drive whenever she heard the sound of a car slowing down. She was hoping the three boys would be coming too, and her vigil was finally rewarded. Mrs Elaman insisted that they have afternoon tea and the children were delighted to have icecream sodas. Gam and Jenny and Mrs Elaman chatted easily and Frances felt her heart do a skip when Gam reminded them of the date for the picnic and jetboat ride at Coppers. Once in the car the boys were full of excitement to tell Frances about their neat Christmas presents, tripping over superlatives to describe the horse, the saddle and the canoe.

Finally their mother shushed them to a quieter murmur, claiming they would give Gam a headache. Gam drove easily and the big car cut out the miles quickly. At Coppers Gam got out and the boys politely carried her parcels. Frances helped too, but as she walked on to the sunporch her heart beat dizzily with earlier memories for a moment. There was no sign of Ian and she had deliberately refrained from asking Gam about him. She was glad when Jenny slipped into the driver's seat and negotiated the drive through the tree tunnel, the darkness hiding her face. Within a few minutes they had reached home and the boys sped out, pulling her in three different directions at once. Despite herself Frances laughed merrily, then diplomatically suggested she looked at the closest treasures first. This was Thad's canoe stored at the side of the garage. She clapped appreciatively as Thad demonstrated the way to port it easily and how to paddle.

'Please say you'll take me down the river sometimes, Frances. I'm not allowed in the main stream, just the side ribbons and only when there's an adult around.' He sighed. 'Mum can't at the moment and Dad and Uncle Ian are always busy. I've had it in the swimming pool and that's neat fun,' his dark eyes glowed and for a second it reminded Frances of Ian.

'Of course I will, Thad, providing I get my work done,' she said, much to the delight of the boy in front of her.

Then it was Ivan the Terrible's turn at showing his saddle, a 'proper grown up' one with spaces for saddlebags and stirrups that glowed with polishing. He smiled proudly and said Frances could borrow it one day if she wanted to, and then Greg was tugging her hand to come to see his horse. An attractive small mare grazed in the paddock, and Greg visibly swelled with pride as she came trotting over to her young master. He was all for demonstrating that he didn't even need a saddle or a bridle, but Frances cuddled his small figure and reminded him of his town clothes. To cheer him she praised the beautiful little chestnut mare extravagantly and told Greg he could go round the stock the next morning if he was up early enough.

The boys danced a series of movements of joy back to the house and were quite willing to go to bed after 'Superman', so they could rise early the next day. As they rode out together in the early morning light Frances glimpsed the excitement in their three faces. Work around the farm had been continuing while she had her holiday. The two big flat paddocks on which Rupert had tried an experimental crop had been harvested in her absence and Thad told her his father had been pleased with the results. When they came to a free flat paddock they all pulled up and she asked Greg to show what his horse could do. He dazzled them with fast runs and neat side steps and even Ivan and Thad were impressed. The mare had such a lovely nature she seemed to enter into the fun too. She tossed her head as though to say, 'I'm better than you,' and they all laughed. Obviously Jenny and Rupe had exercised great care in selecting their youngest son's horse. When they raced together down the paddock Frances noted that now all three boys kept together and Greg's face was red with pride.

It was lunchtime before they reached home as they had shifted some sheep and with all their merriment it had taken much longer than usual. After lunch Frances baked some cakes for Jenny, then peeled some vegetables. The boys helped with these and to reward them Frances said she would take the canoe to the river. Just as the second cake was pulled from the oven Jenny got up so she suggested they take the Land Rover and sling the canoe on to the back. They were made even happier when she said she would come too, and it was a cheerful group that bumped and crashed its way down the farm track to the river. They took the short cut through the grounds of Coppers and Frances remembered well the last time she had been this way. She was glad that driving the Land Rover demanded so much of her effort. It was a new experience for her and she wasn't altogether sure she liked it. The boys made rude remarks when she sent them spinning into each other's laps, until she reached the even path. She was glad Jenny was more comfortable, sitting smilingly in the front seat.

The river looped crazily over small stones in front of them. Today it looked placid and calm, though there was a hint of its force in the farthest stream. Closer to hand it had split itself into three streams and one of these formed a wide pool before rejoining the second stream much further down. Soon Thad was paddling up and down the pool; practising in the swimming pool at home had given him some ability, and he showed his prowess at paddling upstream before letting Ivan have a turn. Greg danced impatiently beside them, not caring that he was splashing water, but his turn eventually came. Surprisingly he seemed to manage even better than Ivan and he turned the boat quite neatly.

Jenny suggested to Thad that Frances have a turn and he handed her into the small canoe rather carefully. Frances' boating expeditions had been limited to paddling a rowboat on the Avon a few times, but it was just as safe in this tiny obliging stream. She was surprised at how much room she had and wiggled herself into position. Thad let go and she paddled cautiously into the current. She backed the canoe round and laughed with the boys when she found herself turning the wrong way. Then she figured it out and really enjoyed herself, realising she could become as big an addict as the boys. Jenny regretfully eyed herself, openly regretting that she wouldn't fit, and Thad promised her two turns after the baby was born.

'At the moment I feel the size of the mountains—well, not quite, perhaps Pudding Hill,' she quipped, and they laughed again.

Ivan gave his mother a consoling hug, then took his turn at the boat. Thad made them have strict rotation and watching him Frances saw how like his father he really was. Jenny nodded, catching her eye and sharing the thought.

The sun was low in the sky when hunger finally drove them home. To disguise the bumps in the track they sang 'Pop goes the Weasel', the boys excitedly cheering when they finally crawled home. Jenny put on dinner immediately and Frances was glad it was all prepared. As they were finishing Rupe and Ian came in. Both looked bone tired and filthy, and Frances longed to hold Ian to her to comfort him and caress away the frown on his forehead.

Since Christmas he seemed to have aged, and contrasting her memory of the sleek, urbane figure with the weary, unkept, dirty man in front of her Frances felt her heart soften with tenderness. Jenny asked him to stay, but he replied that Gam was expecting him. He seemed ill at ease for the first time since Frances had known him, and she felt it was her presence which caused it. Rupe came back with some papers which Ian had wanted, apparently, and he glanced through them, then said goodnight. His glance at Frances seemed disinterested and casual and she staggered under it. She clenched her fists to control the feelings that sent the blood pounding to her forehead, then she was aware of Ian striding off. Too late she realised she had not thanked him for his Christmas gift, although one part of her was glad. She wanted to be alone with Ian when she said thank you. On that thought she felt warmed, and the memory of that casual glance didn't hurt so much. Another small memory tugged at her too. Ian had his shirt open and gleaming against his bronze skin was the silver St Christopher medallion.

The few days after New Year passed quickly. Jenny was feeling most uncomfortable so Frances worked even harder around the house as well as doing her farm work. Finally Jenny remonstrated with her, urging her to relax but she told her it was a way to make up for the trouble over her leg. Each night Rupe came in late and Jenny would look hopefully for rain clouds. 'I hope it rains soon, Rupe and Ian are pushing themselves so hard. Thank God for Sunday and your parents coming.'

On Saturday morning Frances left the farm early and with expert driving had rejoined her family for morning tea. She was relieved that she had managed the trip so easily, her ankle not troubling her at all. Mr and Mrs Elaman were going out visiting an old friend and Frances agreed to take Kathy to the beach. She had left her bikini at the farm, but found an old swimsuit tucked away and tried it on. It still fitted, but looking at herself in the mirror Frances knew she hadn't put on any weight. Her bones were not very flattering and she determined to try to eat a little more. She pulled on a beach-robe and her big beach towel and walked out to the Mini.

They headed through quiet tree-lined streets until they joined the main stream of traffic, following the coast road towards Sumner. This time the tide was in, so they parked beside Cave Rock. The surf today was non-existent, the waves having gone to sleep, lazily licking the sand. After a swim in the sun warmed water Kathy sun-bathed and Frances climbed the nearby landmark of Cave Rock. By the mast on top she perched and watched the flight of the gulls wheeling and screaming for scraps. They reminded her of the gulls at the Rakaia and a glimpse of Ian's face struck at her memory. She stood up to banish the picture and watched the birds again. Occasionally she saw a pied oyster-catcher, its long legs distinctive. Frances climbed down from her perch and with her beach robe over her slim form walked away from the crowds.

Her hair was beginning to dry and she felt its curls bounce on her shoulder. She remembered the way Ian wove it round his fingers and brushed it away, furious with herself for allowing his memory to torment her. She just about tripped over Kathy's recumbent form and apologised to another figure as she sprayed it with sand. A shell attracted her attention and she stooped to pick it up, admiring its shading from cream to amber. Some of the other delicate shells she picked up too and put in her pocket; the boys would enjoy making things with them one wet day. The tide was going out now, leaving more shells behind and she picked up an unusual one in a deep orange colour. Her inspection showed her a tiny creature occupied it so she set it back into the sand. In a small tidal pool trapped by the rock she could see some other shells and she bent to retrieve one. As she did so she noted a tiny starfish blending beautifully with the sand of the pool. She examined it in detail, enthralled with her find, and signalled to Kathy. That young lady was too lazy to move, merely waving a nonchalant arm, evidently considering her sunbathing of more importance. Frances continued her walk, her hazel eyes reflecting the colours around her of sand and sea. Her path was isolated now, only the sea birds keeping her company. In one corner she noticed some strange birds with unusual beaks. She crept closer moving quietly so she would not disturb them. Now she was certain she was watching the bar-tailed godwits. Her father had been quite a student of birds and she remembered the magical day she had seen them as a child. He had called them the travellers and told her that in March or April they would fly in great chevron patterns across the world to Canada or Siberia. Looking at their stance as they fed greedily they seemed quite plump and ordinary, only their beaks extraordinarily deft as they flicked the shellfish out.

Most of the birds filling the skies now were the white terns and the red-billed gulls, still screaming insults. One came closer to her, cawing loudly, and she smiled. He hardly qualified as a singing bird, she thought. Reluctantly she turned back, her thoughts of Ian a dim pain. She knew he would be working hard, the weather was still fine, and she glanced round at the sky hoping it would still be fine in the morning.

CHAPTER NINE

IT WAS a glorious morning and gave promise of another pleasant day as Frances, Martin and Kathy drove to the farm in the Mini. Mr and Mrs Elaman followed in their own car and they made good time reaching Coppers. Before they approached Frances slowed, allowing her parents to see the full beauty of the trees from this angle. Martin and Kathy were vastly impressed with the tree tunnel and Kathy was quietly polite to Gam when she greeted them. Frances smiled at Kathy, understanding the awed silence of her usually irrepressible sister. Seeing the family's interest, Gam showed them the main downstairs rooms and then took them to an outdoors table all ready arranged for a meal. Frances wondered where Ian was and only relaxed when told he would be joining them later in the afternoon.

Conversation flowed easily in the lovely sunny spot dappled by a giant copper beech tree. Dinner was very relaxed and Frances helped Gam clear away, then Gam guided them through the garden on to a park-like area and from there into an orchard filled with a variety of fruit trees. Frances noticed some much younger Cox's Orange apple trees and wondered if Ian had planted them. A line of old walnuts formed a sturdy windbreak and they strolled by it admiring the grouping of the nine large leaves and the fat green globes holding the nuts. Gam explained that they sold a lot of nuts in the past, but now Ian left a lot to the local Boy Scout pack. Dotted throughout were the giant copper beech trees and an ocasional magnificent liquid amber, red oak, lime or ash. Gam told them how her grandfather had loved the English trees and had cuttings and seeds ordered. Owing to a mistake the only trees to arrive were the copper beeches, so he had planted them and only much later were the others added. Seeing the colours of the original trees, he and his wife had deliberately arranged the kaleidoscope of colour that now was so admired. Their son and his wife had added more, including the fine drive which swept up to the house. Gam pointed out lots of details that a casual observer would have missed. She seemed to know each tree, its botanical name, who had planted it and when. Gam herself had planted an impressive number and had built up a section of natives in another part. A group of kowhais was her special gift to the beauty around her, and it stirred Frances to know that generations ahead would admire these beautiful golden-flowering trees.

They wandered quietly back to the house and made ready for the trip to the river. Jenny, Rupe and the boys were to join them down there. From the farmhouse the track ran down to the river. Frances was very familiar with it now and she opened the gates for Gam to drive through. The stock looked as good as on Rupe's side and her eye picked up the crop of white clover waiting in the sun.

With a final bump they pulled up by the riverbank. Gam parked the car under a nearby tree for shade. They all helped to carry the barbecue and picnic gear down to a spot Gam pointed out. Mr Elaman put some bottles into one of the streams of the river to keep cool; they would be appreciated later. From here the river stretched out over a stony bed. As though wriggling to get comfortable the river had bent and twisted itself into a myriad silver-blue channels, leaving odd patches of sand and shingle. The party settled behind a bank as it gave them shelter from the wind. It was one of the few areas free of boulders and a couple of old willows formed a handy backrest. They were just finishing adjusting the rugs when the cries of the boys announced the arrival of the Marsden family. The children raced off to get Thad's canoe and they took it in turn to paddle in the large pool in front of them. While they were waiting they searched for unusual stones and soon they had a heap of 'treasure'. Occasionally the roar of a jetboat sounded in the distance from the main bed of the river as someone headed for a pet fishing spot. From this viewpoint they looked like giant fish perpetually poised to skim over the water. Overhead a couple of large black-backed gulls wheeled, catching Mr Elaman's attention. He commented on them and Jenny laughed at his expression when she told him there was a ledge up in the Gorge where they nested each season.

'I'll ask Ian to point it out to you when he takes you up there this afternoon.' Conversation was desultory, everyone enjoying the clean fresh air and the scent of the broom on the bank behind them. Frances lay back on the rug, content to watch the clouds form patterns that chased each other across the sky. When she moved her head, her eye was caught by the movement of a small bird. It was a tiny fantail and its glinting bright eye peeped at Frances. She lay very still watching it in delight. It was quite small, its distinctive tail opening and shutting rapidly as its name suggested. Its aerobatics were skilfully executed, its tail acting at times like a rudder in the air. It seemed quite fearless, hopping cheekily to an even lower branch, and Frances was able to appreciate the soft copper bronze feathers on its breast and the tonings of dark brown wing feathers. As the tail fanned open and shut a flash of white glistened among the black feathers. It gave a quick 'cheep, cheep' and disappeared just as swiftly as it had come.

She looked around her appreciatively, noting yet again the loveliness of the spot. The giant chain of the mountains were snowcapped, seeming an impenetrable barrier to the land beyond. She could follow the line of the river right up to where it disappeared in a haze of green. A jetboat came downstream, dancing skittishly from the main river into one of the narrow side streams. The easy way the boat handled the fast running water surprised her. She knew it was Ian driving it, even from this distance, and she watched as he brought the boat right up to the bank.

He jumped out with the ease of one who has done it hundreds of times and Martin and Rupe helped him pull the boat higher. He greeted them all cheerfully and Frances was pleased to see he looked less tired than the last time she had seen him, after haymaking. His smile flashed at her spontaneously and she felt reassured by the lightning glance. It had been arranged that Gam, Jenny and Rupe and the boys would light a fire and put a billy on while the Elaman family went for a ride. Thanks to the positioning of the boat on the bank it was surprisingly easy to step on board. To Frances' surprise the boat was extremely comfortable, the seats reminding her of car upholstery with their thick padding. The dashboard had several instrument gauges and a keychain swung gently with the movement as they positioned themselves. Rupe pushed the boat back from the bank as Ian turned the key and the motor roared into life. Ian backed the boat and the swirl of water spraying behind them made Frances forget any other transport. Ian took care negotiating the stream as there was barely enough water to clear the boat. The water was astonishingly close, almost as if they were sitting in it, then the prow lifted as the water pressure altered. The boat responded to Ian's touch as they reached the main stream in a shower of diamond sparkles freed from the confining restrictions, and they skimmed along the surface.

Frances stood at the rail, her eyes reflecting the exhilaration she felt. The speed and grace of the boat in its right element had to be experienced. From the main current the water was a fabulous aqua blue turning to jade, then splashing silver. Feeling the wind whip through her hair, she half shuttered her eyes so she could see the colours of the river. Now she had time to look about her to appreciate the changing contours of the countryside. The width of the river had startled her. From the far bank of the farm she had not realised quite how vast the river was. She seemed surrounded by paddocks of gravel, split neatly by the shining streams. Occasionally Ian would swing the boat towards one of the smaller streams and Frances would hold her breath as he gunned the motor to clear the rise. It was incredible how little water the jetboat needed, and the smoothness of the ride was surprising. Ian mainly followed the edge of the main stream, thus giving the smoothest surface to the passengers. They turned a corner and could see banks of cliffs heading towards the gorge. Ian pulled over a few minutes later so they could see the Highbank Power Station located like some ancient fortress on one bank, pylons legging it across the river carrying the power to the main grid. A little farther up, a second set of steel arms upheld the power from the mighty Benmore power scheme in the south.

A touch of Ian's foot and away they shot, arrow-swift, skirting an island made by the river, swinging the boat back on itself in an elegant manoeuvre that startled them. Ian's grin as he angled the boat sharply to head upstream again showed how much he enjoyed showing off the abilities of the boat. Mr Elaman pointed out a yellow line etched sharply against the grey cliffs, rising steeply now, and Ian agreed that it was a seam of lime. Frances noticed the colour of the water ran a darker green as the streams met and combined into a deep surging mass. They were approaching the Gorge now and Frances noticed several fishermen all hoping to catch a salmon. Ian told Mrs Elaman that the spot was greatly favoured by the fishermen and that sometimes there were so many the locals referred to their appearance as 'a picket fence'. Ian cut the motor so he would not disturb them and Frances had time to see the spars of the old bridge above them. It formed a tracery of geometric design against the backdrop of the river, the green of the bush screening the cliffs and a towering backdrop, the pile of Mount Hutt, its top covered in cloud.

'The bridge was built in 1883,' Ian explained. 'For its day it was quite a remarkable piece of engineering. They bought most of it out here on traction engines and bullock wagons. Before the bridge was built a ferryman used to take people and stock across. I'll point it out as we go through.'

The cliffs were high above them and there was little similarity in this solid torrent to the lazy river of the plains that Frances knew. She was barely aware of the speeding boat, the new sensations of speed and water and wave having heightened all awareness of the vast beauty around.

A tiny waterfall spurted jets of water, making silver sprays in the sunlight as it fell down the bank towards the river. The bush gradually fell away as Ian pointed out a bare ledge.

'The seagulls' rookery.' He angled the boat and cut the motor to a barely throbbing idle so they could appreciate the scene. Stark shingle cliffs towered above them to the sky. The wind moaned around them, chasing small spirals of shingle to the river. They had been carved into strange shapes, and Frances shivered with the realisation of the years it must have taken. They could hear the steady rattle as stones continually fell, cascading occasionally as a bigger section hit the river below.

She was glad that Ian revved the boat and they swung away, heading further upstream. Soon a group of lovely old trees on the terraced farmlands on the opposite side caught her eye and reminded her briefly of Coppers. A homestead was enclosed in its shelter. Ian turned the boat as they followed the curve of the river and they gasped in amazement. They seemed to be isolated in the middle of a primeval world, surrounded by mountains. The sun shone down, and it seemed much warmer up here than in the plains below.

'It looks as if we're in the middle of a giant's mixing bowl,' put in Kathy.

'This was part of a glacier, aeons ago,' said Ian. 'If you look at the rock patterns on the cliffs you can see the different lake levels quite clearly. As the glacier receded the water forced a way through the rocks, forming today's Gorge. The plains are still being built up by the river's flow today.'

'Gee! Oh! Wow!' was Kathy's awed comment, and it seemed to express quite a lot.

Ian glanced at his watch and said they should turn back. Frances was surprised how long they had been, time had passed so quickly. Heading downstream the boat slapped the water rhythmically, and they enjoyed Ian's handling of the boat, making it seem ridiculously easy as they angled round corners. Showers of silver sparkled briefly as they met a series of rapids, Frances clutching on to the handrail as they swooped and dived. They shot under the bridge then slowed past the fishermen still standing in a hopeful vigil. The sunlight flashed on them again as the river opened out green-blue on the piles of grey stones.

Looking up, Frances noticed two large attractive modern buildings placed near a side road above the river. Her mother had noticed too and Ian told her it was the Mount Hutt Lodge, placed ideally for skiers, trampers and fishermen. Set in the valley, it must have a glorious outlook across the river to Mount Hutt, thought Frances.

Soon they were speeding past the power station, Ian pointing out the pipe that brought water from the irrigation scheme on the other side. The river began its lazy meandering again and once again the jetboat leapt to the challenge it offered. No wonder Ian loved this sport, thought Frances. It was so raw and elemental, and she glanced up at him, seeing the expression on his face, now as hooded and silent as the mountains behind them. Clouds covered the sun momentarily and Frances was staggered at the change in the scene, the colours having been bleached suddenly into a world of grey stones, grey sky and grey river. She was glad of the warmth of the lifejacket and sat down against the comfortable seat. Ian waved to a fisherman who proudly held a large shimmering fish he had just pulled from the river.

Then the clouds moved on and the sun shone through, transforming the scene into its bright glinting colours. A trail of smoke drifted skywards and with a pang Frances realised she was on familiar territory again. The boys ran to meet them as they pulled up and Rupe helped to pull the boat higher so they could step out more easily. The touch of Ian's hand as she stepped off the boat sent the colour flying from her face. She thanked him, breathlessly glad she could, then turned to help her parents.

'That was the thrill of a lifetime!' said Mrs Elaman. 'That was terrific, Ian.'

'Gee, I'm hungry!' said Kathy, reducing the rarefied atmosphere in one healthy remark.

The boys had built a fire among the stones and Jenny had produced a billy and set it to boil. There was no shortage of fuel, the river had left a line of debris and sticks right on the edge of the bank. The boys showed Kathy how to build the stone fireplace, delighted to be able to show off their superior knowledge. The billy tea was delicious and despite the large lunch they had eaten earlier, the food disappeared quickly. The river had whipped up all their appetites. Then Ian took Kathy and the boys for a run in the boat while they cleaned up. Rupe showed them a spot in the bank where some Maori ovens had been exposed by the recent floods. The early Maoris had hunted the giant moa which had roamed this area then rafted the huge bodies downstream to their more sheltered campsites. Frances walked closer and could make out the outline still but little else from this angle. She gathered more driftwood for the barbecue that Rupe and her father were already setting up. Soon they had quite a decent fire going and a ready pile of logs and sticks. Gam pulled out a large cast-iron griddle which must have been used in the early days for cooking out at the farm. It sat neatly on a tripod over the glowing embers and the fire was built up on the other side.

Ian bought the boat back under a darkening sky, the children full of its delight. Rupe helped him load it on to the trailer hooked on to the Land Rover. Gam had placed foil-wrapped potatoes in the ashes earlier and now she scooped them to the edge where they could keep hot but not overcook. The meat was sizzling and the fires of the barbecue lit the faces gathered around. Frances took the billy and walked over to a fast-running stream to fill it carefully. Ian took it from her and swung it into place on a low hook. The flames cast strange shadows across his face as she met his eyes, but she turned away quickly, not willing to let her feelings be shown. She found the bottles her father had laid down in the pool earlier and there was a hilarious moment as the top of one sailed out to hit a branch. The second bottle was managed with much more expertise, much to the boys' and Kathy's disappointment. They started their own game of targets, using a log in the stream and a pile of stones. The fact that they could hardly see the target seemed to add to their hilarity.

The barbecued food was delicious and the light wine added to the effervescence of the occasion. Someone started singing and gradually the whole party joined in with pop songs as well as old folk songs. Frances pressed her father to do his party piece, 'O Sole Mio'. It was very familiar to all the Elaman family, being one of the few Frances' father knew by heart. He had quite a pleasant voice and the richness of the Italian floated across the river. Too late Frances remembered Gam, and she hoped it would not disturb her when it was finished. She touched her arm sympathetically, but Gam smilingly reassured her.

'You're right, my dear, but it's a joy to think of happy times. Perhaps in later years today will be a golden memory for you.'

Frances nodded slowly. There had been something special about today. Her eyes looked up at Ian chatting easily to her mother and Thad. She glanced away as they joined in singing a Neil Diamond hit. She watched him, glad to be inked out of the light so she could study his face unobserved. He stood up and made coffee for anyone who wanted it, then brought her a cup and sat beside her. His hand held hers briefly before he began singing the mournful ballad of poor Clementine. Everyone joined in the chorus, but Ian seemed to know all the verses and at the end was roaring them out, much to the delight and approval of the youngsters, who had obviously not heard the old song before.

It was time to pack up. The fire was almost out when Frances said goodbye to her parents, Gam taking them back to Coppers. Frances was about to go with them, but Ian asked if she would ride with him so he would have help with the gates. So much for wanting her company, she thought wryly. Soon all the cars were loaded and Jenny waved in farewell. Frances watched as Ian trod out the remaining embers, then poured water on to the fire. Without the cheerful fire it looked eerie and strange, and she shivered suddenly. Ian came up and put his coat around her and she thanked him gravely, trying to keep emotion under control. They climbed up the bank, Ian supporting her, and she was glad of his assistance. The Land Rover stood like some monolithic structure, with the boat as a curious appendage.

Ian opened the door for her and she climbed in, thinking it was impossible to do so elegantly. They bounced around in the seat, the lights piercing the darkness ahead of them. At the gate Frances hopped down and Ian drove through, wordlessly changing over for the next one. He expertly pulled the Land Rover up as they reached Coppers, neatly reversing the boat on its trailer into the garage. There was no sign of her parents; they must have left immediately.

Gam had left an outside light on and it shone down on her Mini. Stiffly Frances stepped down and moved towards it. Ian was busy unhooking the Land Rover and she saw him remove the holding pin and gently bed the trailer. It occurred to her that it was a good time to thank Ian for her Christmas present, even if its message seemed contradictory. She had noted that Ian wore his silver St Christopher still and it gave her courage to approach him now.

He stood easily, his eyes shielded from her so she could not read their expression as she slipped her hands around his neck. She kissed him gently, explaining that it was a thank-you for her Christmas present. The brief touch of their bodies sparked an instant reaction and she was blissfully aware of Ian's kisses crushing her, seeking a response from her trembling body.

He pushed her away and she saw his face in the light for a second as he struggled for control, his hands clenching tightly at his side and his stance stiff. Then he relaxed with a lazy laugh 'That's some thank-you, water baby! Go on home. I'm not the one to make the singing bird come.' He climbed back into the Land Rover as Frances opened the Mini, her legs barely supporting her. Mechanically she drove it out of the yard and down the tree tunnel where the tears poured down her face.

She sniffed inelegantly, hastily trying to stop crying. Ruefully she grimaced at her own temerity. If only Ian's physical presence didn't send her pulses soaring everything would be so easy. Well, at least now she knew she was no longer an empty box elegantly wrapped but a throbbing vital woman who wanted to be loved by her man. She parked the Mini and straightened her shoulders unconsciously, her light suitcase in her hand. Jenny and Rupe were still up, probably putting the children to bed. Greg was sitting up at the kitchen table, his eyes large in the dim light as he slowly stirred a hot chocolate drink. His brothers must have finished theirs, as there was no sign of them.

'Did Ian put the fire out? Did it take a long time?' he asked anxiously as she walked in.

'The fire? Oh, you mean the bonfire at the river.' Frances took a moment to gather her thoughts. 'Oh, Ian put it out quite easily. He scattered it, tramped on it and poured water on it. The smoke and steam showed for a minute and then it was quite dead, not even an ember left.' Like me, she said to herself, bitterly recalling his rejection.

Greg sighed. 'That's good! When I grow up I'm going to be just like Dad and Uncle Ian.' He slurped his cocoa slowly, before putting the mug on the bench and kissing her goodnight. She kissed him gently, then he ran off down the hall to his bedroom. His gesture cheered her, the loving affectionate touch was so warm and comforting. In bed, though, it turned to bitter ashes as she realised that she would not know the joy of children of her own. She had never met a man like Ian before and she doubted if anyone else would be able to brighten the stars for her. Bitterly she recalled his message of the singing bird, yet he had killed her hopes mercilessly by saying that he was not the one to make the singing bird come.

Frances settled in bed, pulling the sheet around her despite the heat of the night. If it wasn't for Jenny, Rupe and the children she would leave tomorrow, but this was a situation she had to live through in her own private anguish. She couldn't abandon Jenny now with the birth so close, and Rupe would miss her help with the pastures and stock. She had to stay even if it meant suffering the agony of seeing the man she loved ignoring her completely.

She dressed carefully, brushing her hair into a pile of

red-gold curls on top of her head. It was far too formal for everyday, but she felt she needed every shred of pride she could find to help stiffen her morale. Jenny and Rupe were having breakfast, and their closeness sent a shaft of pain into her being. Rupe commented on her hair; it was rare indeed for him to make a personal comment and she thanked him briefly.

'Should I get jealous?' Jenny laughed.

'Oh yes, please,' said Rupe. 'I'd love to have my wife make mad, passionate love to me.'

He reached over and kissed her soundly as the toast popped. Jenny's eyes glowed as she looked at her husband. The boys must have decided on a sleep-in for a change, Frances thought; usually they were up waiting to ride out with her. Soon they would be going on their holiday with Gam. Frances knew she would miss the boys, their constant companionship had kept her mind from floating off to thoughts of Ian.

It was a beautiful morning, with almost no wind, as Frances cantered around the paddocks. She changed the irrigation as Rupe had advised then headed off to the river flat. In the morning light the scene was a delight. She followed the fence line down to the river, noting the crop of white clover on either side. Here and there a crop of boulders and stones had been gathered into odd cairn-like shapes, a reminder of the river not far away. The sheep grazed quietly. Greytor moved softly and rhythmically along until Frances pulled her up beside a gap in the fence. A tuft of wool fluttered a white signal at the edge of one wire. She swung herself down, greatly to Scamp's delight, and tied Greytor to a handy willow.

It was impossible from here to see if many sheep had gone through the gap. The bank was higher here and she followed it along, knowing the sheep would seek an easy route down. A grin flashed across her face as she recognised the path as the one she had taken on that day she had paddled and Ian had found her.

A couple of bleats caught her ear and she saw two sheep stuck out on a shingle island. They had made their way over a narrow neck and after finding the lupins not to their taste had not been able to find the way back. Frances sighed. It was a lot easier to shift a hundred sheep in this terrain than two who could dart in any direction. Scamp barked in enthusiasm, his tail forming an eager question mark. Frances wondered if she should leave the sheep there and go back to get Fay. This was a situation that demanded a good dog. Scamp was far too young to handle them. Perhaps if she could grab one she could guide it to the bank and throw it over the fence at the top. The other might follow, she thought optimistically.

She studied the path the sheep had used. If she approached that way she ran the risk of sending the sheep into the river on one side or the pool on the other. However, if she approached from the pool end the sheep might just go straight down the shingle neck and on to the path. Regretfully she eyed her jeans, then she rolled them up above the knee and stepped into the pool. It was icy cold but not very deep. Scamp looked at her pleadingly, then decided he would follow causing a shower of spray as he shook himself on the island. The plan began to succeed. The sheep, seeing her, fled in the other direction straight along the path. Scamp, however, raced along and cut them off and Frances had to recall him. She couldn't be angry with him when he stood, tail wagging and head cocked, as though to say, 'Didn't I do well?' Frances chuckled despite her plan being upset and Scamp raced back to her. The sheep, considerably startled, raced back the other way. Frances kept a tight hold of Scamp, much to his indignation, and tried to guide the sheep slowly but steadily towards the path. She found it difficult, however, as Scamp wriggled and danced under her fingers. She let him go, hoping he had learnt his lesson, but in one bound he had sent the sheep skittering again and one headed for the pool. Instinctively Frances splashed in, rapidly hoisting her jeans above her knees. The sheep turned and dashed back. Frances called Scamp to sit and he obeyed for once, enabling her to move quietly up by the sheep. One of them, cornered, turned to face her, bravely tapping the ground with a raised foot. Smiling, Frances wished she had a dog to go round the other side. As though her wish had been granted there was Ian's dog looking at her, for a command. It was the work of only a minute to get the sheep into the path and climbing rapidly up the bank. They even struggled through the gap in the fence under the watchful eyes of Blackie and Scamp.

Frances patted Blackie thankfully, then watched as he streaked towards the willows where a tall figure leaned lazily. Frances stiffened, instinctively pulling at her jeans.

'Wait, dry those gorgeous legs first or you'll feel uncomfortable,' came the familiar mocking voice.

He walked over to her, a large neatly folded handkerchief in his hand. Ruefully Frances took it and dried her legs, acutely aware of his gaze. She unrolled her jeans and stood facing him. Her pulses raced as she felt the impact of his gaze. She was glad that Scamp barked, attracting their attention. Ian turned towards his motorbike. 'Actually you handled that quite well once Blackie was there. Scamp's got a good heart, but he's too young, only nuisance value at the moment.'

'High praise, sir,' Frances grinned at him cheekily. 'Thanks for sending Blackie. I'd probably still be there otherwise.'

'Very likely,' he said, eyeing her. 'Come here and I'll show you where we keep some gear.' He held out his hand and she took it naturally as he pushed a way to the boundary fence. His grip was iron-hard and she was glad of the support as they leapt over lupins and old logs. With one foot on a log she slipped as it rolled and she clutched on to Ian for support. His other arm enfolded her naturally and his eyes darkened as his mouth sought hers in a deep searing kiss.

'Oh, water baby!' he muttered, then turned resolutely to a box hidden at the base of a willow by the fence. Frances watched as he opened the box, pulled out a length of wire and a wire strainer and a hammer and staples. She noticed rope and anchor pins and some other tools neatly bound in plastic too.

Ian strode ahead of her to the gap, this time not offering her a hand to scramble over the lupins and logs. She waited patiently as he tightened the two wires and took up the slack. 'I'll fix this. You might as well go back, water baby. Our paths lie in different directions.'

She climbed on to Greytor, hearing his curt dismissal ring in her ear. She ached, feeling again the way her body had reacted to his kiss, knowing that he too felt the passion that always flared between them. She heard the sound of hammering behind her and sent Greytor flying with her sudden urging to leave. By the time she reached the farmhouse most of the tension had left her and she was glad to be able to face the boys with some equanimity. They were cleaning the shed for their father and were delighted to stop work, obviously not enjoying their task. Frances helped them with it, then went swimming with them, much to their delight. That night she told Rupe about the fence and mentioned that Ian had fixed it. He gazed at her briefly, then nodded.

The boys accompanied Frances round the stock, in the morning, and what with dogs and ponies, it was quite a trek. Rupe had left instructions to shift a mob and they worked together in the freshness of the day. Fay made a wide cast to round up the stragglers, gathering them into a neat mob. Scamp joined in, his bark sounding eagerly as he ran back and forth, making up in noise what he lacked in sense. However, he obeyed her whistles and with Fay on the spot they had no difficulty. Thad and Greg rode to the gate and opened it, standing guard to make a quick count. Frances went to stand beside them and she angled the gate further. Thad might be able to count six or seven sheep at a time, but she certainly couldn't. She signalled Ivan to send the mob through and concentrated very hard on her count. Ivan did his job steadily, moving the mob evenly through the gap. At the finish Frances checked numbers with Thad and was delighted they had the same. It tallied with the numbers there were meant to be, so she knew no others had escaped through the gap yesterday.

She looked at the fence. It stood taut and even, so Ian had done a good job. Somehow the knowledge irked her, and she urged Greytor into a quick gallop. The children wheeled their mounts, thinking it was a race, and they set off in hot pursuit. Their laughter on reaching the water race at the next paddock diverted her thoughts.

In two days' time the boys would be leaving for their holidays, so when they returned to the house Frances was not surprised to see Jenny busy packing their clothes. The tiny shorts and shirts, socks and underwear had been checked earlier. The boys were taking one game each in case of wet days. Frances made them some cakes that afternoon. The boys' appetites were prodigious and the cake tins were always emptied quickly. No doubt Gam had done some baking too, but it wouldn't be wasted, thought Frances. Thad and Ivan were full of excitement, discussing aspects of the trip, so that Greg listened slightly wide-eyed. He was uncertain, obviously, yet delighted at being considered a 'big' boy, able to go on holiday. Frances heard Jenny reassure him that Uncle Ian would drive up one day.

'I'll ask him to stay, Mum. Do you think he will?'

'Well, he might, Greg, if you ask him nicely.'

Overhearing this comment made Frances smile. Ian was greatly loved by his small nephews and he would no doubt stay if they needed him. He had such a natural way with children, she reflected. Desperately she wished she wasn't in love with him. She knew from his words and his immediate withdrawal from those kisses that there was no future in their relationship. For a few moments she dared to dream what would happen if Ian loved her. However, reality intruded abruptly with Ivan swearing he hadn't pinched Thad's socks and Thad's angry reply. Frances smiled as Greg timidly proffered her the missing garments and she put an end to the fight.

CHAPTER TEN

THE boys had their last ride before the holidays and cleaned and shone their gear. Much to their disgust, they had to tidy their rooms, and for a short time there were quite a lot of 'That's yours!' and 'Look what I've found' type comments.

Frances and Jenny had morning tea together, wisely letting the boys sort their treasures alone. By lunchtime the rooms looked presentable and their suitcases stood ready.

Looking down the hall, Frances smiled as a suitcase showed from every door except hers! Jenny laughed too; her bag had been packed much earlier just in case she had to go to the maternity hospital. The boys had given her strict instructions to bring home a girl, Thad being the only one to contemplate another boy with any degree of complacency. Although little had been said on the topic Frances knew well just how much Jenny and Rupe were hoping for a girl too.

Gam arrived on the dot of eight in the morning, the boys waiting eagerly. This morning Rupe had waited to say goodbye and breakfast had been a particularly busy time. Thad and Ivan were seething with excitement and they clambered eagerly into the car, stopping only to kiss their parents in a brief flurry. Greg parted from them somewhat reluctantly, then joined the others, and finally managed a smile, much to his mother's relief. They waved as the car moved down the drive and out on to the road. Rupe put his arm around his wife and Frances, not wishing to intrude, sped back to the kitchen and put the kettle on.

Rupe pulled down cups too and Jenny soon cheered up. Rupe started telling Frances about the work for that day and she listened attentively as usual, as Rupe told them how he could be contacted if necessary.

Frances delayed her farm work until the boys' bedrooms were tidied. The house seemed so empty. However, Jenny waved her off happily enough later and Frances enjoyed her ride round the farm. As she rode she remembered Ian would be coming to the house more often in the time Gam was away. He was accustomed to baching on his own as Gam was often away, but Jenny had been insistent; she knew how tired the men were during harvesting. Wearily Frances sighed. If only she hadn't complicated things by falling in love with Ian, how much more simple life would be.

She watched as the men came up to the house that night. The light from outside lit the angles of their faces, Rupe's quiet and sturdy, a faint grin on his face as he passed some comment to the smiling man at his side. Ian moved with an easy grace, his laugh sounding natural. Bitterly Frances turned away. He seemed happy enough, she thought ruefully. The men had a quick shower and joined them for dinner. Their efforts had given them healthy appetites and owing to their late start they were remarkably fresh. Frances had become accustomed to having her main meal with the boys and now she had got past her initial hunger. Her appetite had deserted her, but she made a play at eating when she caught Ian's gaze on her. Deliberately no one mentioned the boys after Rupe's earlier enquiry. Earlier Jenny had been full of speculation as to the time of their arrival and when this had long passed Frances knew she was becoming anxious. Gam had promised to ring on arrival at the beach and the delay was unusual. They had almost finished dessert when the phone finally rang and Rupe leapt at it, his well disguised concern showing at last.

It was with a smile he reported that all was well. Gam had suffered the indignity of a flat tyre and had chosen to get it repaired in Motueka before carrying on.

Rupert produced a liqueur with their coffee, Jenny

put her feet up on the couch and her husband, after waiting on her, took the rocking chair. Ian prowled the room uneasily and Frances knew he felt the tension between them. Finally he said he had paperwork to do at home and set off with a casual farewell.

Frances stacked the dishes and set the machine whirring, washing the fine crystal liqueur glasses by hand. She felt strung up herself and wished she could go for a run, but knew it was out of the question.

The morning came at last with clouds and scattered showers. Rupert worked on the farm, so Frances felt free to help Jenny. She roared around the house with the vacuum cleaner, then started on the windows, knowing Jenny usually kept them sparkling. In the afternoon she decided to swim. She had deliberately not gone swimming in the pool until her leg was healed. It was wonderful to feel the water lapping around her and the rain spattering down seemed warm on her skin. Ian was not coming over for a meal that night. He had rung earlier and Frances had heard Jenny talking to him. She wished she had answered the phone, then thrust the thought from her angrily. She swam up and down the pool as quickly as she could and felt easier after the exercise. The clouds had disappeared as the wind had changed and as evening fell it became warm again. During the night the wind kept up and the next morning no evidence of any damp remained. In the afternoon Rupert went over to the harvesting again. Frances was glad to remain with Jenny. Ian came over for a meal, but as they were very late the dinner was eaten quickly and he left immediately afterwards.

The days fell into their pattern, of constant tiring effort. Jenny was feeling fractious as she was overdue and Rupert and Ian were most solicitous for her welfare. Frances split her runs round the stock so that she came back to the house twice. It took more effort, but it was worth it for everyone's peace of mind. The boys sent a regular stream of postcards, of beaches featuring golden white sand. Jenny pinned them on to the wall notice board where normally their school work featured and they formed a bright splash of colour.

Jenny and Rupert's bedroom had the wicker bassinet already set up in one corner, and Jenny's suitcase was standing beside it.

'I'm beginning to feel this baby might be a girl,' laughed Jenny one morning. 'All the boys were punctual to the day, so keep your fingers crossed!'

It was a relief to find Jenny in such a pleasant mood. The last week had been decidedly trying. 'I'm sorry I've been such a bear, but I've been feeling so down in the dumps; this heat has been bugging me. Thank goodness I feel more myself this morning. For the first time I feel as though I've got some energy to do things.'

'Well, just take it quietly, Jenny,' urged Frances. 'I'm off to fix up the irrigation, but I'll be back in an hour.'

'Fine, I might make some scones. Haven't made any since the boys left and I just feel like it this morning.' Frances went off smiling. Greytor, Scamp and Fay were waiting for her and it was the work of a few minutes to saddle up and speed out in the fresh air, the dogs chasing each other as she cantered along. She knew the pattern of work well now, so she was quite surprised to find a mob of sheep in a paddock Rupert had kept shut for late feed. She looked at the sheep and eyed the gate. It was half open. If Rupert had wanted the stock in this paddock surely he would have put the sheep through the gate and closed off the first paddock. The paddock where the sheep had been grazing still had plenty of sweet young grass. Rupert had mentioned having trouble one other day from picnickers who left gates open, allowing stock to become mixed. Because the farm was off the main road they rarely had trouble, but sometimes a group would cut down to the river across the farm. Frances decided to shift the sheep back into the first paddock. Rupert would have told her if he wanted the late feed opened up. It would be easy enough to come down later and open it again if she had been wrong. The dogs made a wide cast round the paddock, Scamp following Fay's lead. The sheep moved out, reluctantly, and Frances was aware of Scamp hurrying them up, his pink tongue flapping and his eyes sparkling. Already his puppy unruliness was disappearing, but Frances made a special point of always teaming him with one of the older dogs. When the mob were back in the paddock she fastened the gate carefully and then sped on with the rest of her work. She glanced at her watch, surprised to see how much time had elapsed. She was almost at the river flats and to have to return would mean a much longer journey later on. Fortunately, everything else was as it was meant to be, so she made up some time galloping Greytor home again.

As she walked into the house the aroma of freshly made scones greeted her. To her surprise they were still on the oven tray on top of the stove. Jenny normally placed them on a clean linen teatowel and wrapped them in an ovencloth to keep hot. Frances went to the bathroom and washed herself thoroughly, then went back to the kitchen to put the kettle on.

There was no sign of Jenny; so perhaps she had walked up to get the mail from the box at the road. Frances called and called her name, but still no reply. Still not concerned but thinking it was unlike Jenny, she went through the house, but no sign or sound disturbed the stillness. She glanced round the front garden and then by the pool, then she began running up to the main gate. The mail was still in the box and she felt cold. Something was definitely wrong. The mail would have been there almost half an hour before and Jenny always watched for it eagerly. Telling herself not to panic as there could easily be some simple explanation, Frances sped back to the house. She decided to ring the farm where Rupe was working to get him to come home. To her great relief the phone was answered immediately and the farmer's wife said she would run to tell Rupert straight away.

She heard Scamp barking and wondered what he had found, his excited woofs being joined by the other dogs. Remembering how fond Jenny was of Scamp, Frances ran to investigate, and was greatly relieved to see Jenny sitting with a great bunch of gladioli at the side of the garage.

'Oh, I am so glad to see you—I think I must have fainted. Oh, help!' gasped Jenny as a spasm of pain flooded her. 'Get Rupert quick, Frances!'

She doubled over as she attempted to stand, and gripped Frances very tightly. Then the pain rolled away and she was able to walk towards the house. She had only gone past the garage when she doubled over again. 'I'll never make it. The baby seems to be making up for lost time!'

Frances eased her on to the ground and sped back to the house. She grabbed the car keys and a pile of towels and Jenny's suitcases and ran back and put them in the car. She pulled the car up beside Jenny and was helping her into the back seat when Rupert and Ian arrived. They ran over and quickly Frances told them what she knew. Jenny was again doubled with pain and it was immediately obvious she was in labour.

'Ian, ring the doctor, notify the ambulance to meet us en route and then ring the hospital. Frances, hop in and we'll motor.'

Gently Rupert drove down the metal road, but once on the tarseal he put his foot down. For Frances it was a nightmare; she was vividly aware of her lack of nursing experience.

'Don't worry,' said Rupert, seeing her white, anxious face. 'If I have to I'll be able to help.'

Jenny laughed weakly, then gasped in pain. Rupert slowed as they approached an intersection, then they roared away again. By timing the contractions, Frances doubted if they would make it to the hospital. At least by now the ambulance would be on its way. Ian would have seen to that.

Jenny smiled, a touch of her old self again. 'Look at me—hardly the smartest outfit, but I've bought my flowers! I was picking them for the lounge and I went to the back of the garage to get some of that variegated flax. I remember bending to get some and the baby moved suddenly and I went out like a light.'

'Gladioli—well, perhaps this baby will make you glad,' smiled Frances. She gently wiped away beads of sweat from Jenny's face and eased her over so that she could be more comfortable.

Frances gazed ahead at the straight band of black tarseal, hoping to see the white of the ambulance. At the speed Rupe was travelling the miles to the hospital would be covered in half the usual time. He was concentrating all his energy on driving, and glancing at the speedometer Frances was glad of his skill. She gave Jenny her hand to grip as a spasm of pain shook the heavy body. Jenny sighed, 'I don't think I'll be having this baby in hospital!'

'Still, the ambulance should be meeting us soon,' soothed Frances. She could see the contractions were regular and the pattern of labour had changed. Gently she told Rupe and he slackened speed. Even to stop at the speed they were travelling had to be a gradual process. The last thing they needed was a sudden jolt, thought Frances apprehensively.

Rupe was swearing softly as he dived from the car and opened the boot. He pulled out a large first aid kit and Frances was surprised at the equipment it revealed. He washed his hands and arms liberally in the disinfectant and joked with his wife, apparently calm and at ease. Only the quick anxious glance towards the road showed his strain. Frances felt strange. She knew she was giving Jenny support and while she held on so desperately the tension was broken by the scream of a siren.

The relief they all felt was echoed by Jenny's 'Just in time!' The ambulance staff took over and a few minutes later the baby had made its appearance. Rupert took the tiny wailing scrap of humanity. 'A girl, my love!' His joy showed in the few words as he bent to kiss his wife. Jenny gave the baby to Frances to hold as the men prepared to lift her into the ambulance.

One of the towels she had picked up in that last minute was wrapped round the baby, rather red, its hair looking wetly black against the tiny scalp. The eyes were wrinkled slits, but the incredibly small nose and the delicate ears were so exquisite Frances felt very moved. She looked up at Ian, sharing this very special moment with him. He took the baby from her with a deft gentleness and passed her to Rupe beside his wife in the ambulance.

There was a quick discussion as it was decided that Rupe would follow the ambulance in his own car and Ian would take Frances home.

Ian picked up the first aid box and shoved it back on the seat of the car as his brother-in-law waved a cheerful farewell. Frances watched as the big silver car swung behind the ambulance moving ponderously along.

Suddenly she felt weak and watery-eyed. Everything had happened so quickly, from those first panic-stricken moments of not being able to find Jenny, to the arrival of the baby, that now reaction set in and she shivered with emotion. Ian pulled her close and she leaned against him, grateful for his solid strength. For a few minutes they sat close together and neither spoke. Afterwards Frances realised that Ian was probably feeling just as strained, but she was glad of his silence. Eventually he leant and kissed her forehead, then turned the motor on. There was an easy companionship between them as he drove back towards Coppers. He explained that he had followed them as quickly as he could. 'I didn't think you'd make it in time, so I thought I'd better be there just in case.' The lazy grin was back now and the deep brown eyes held their trace of mischief. He swung into the drive of Coppers with practised skill and the light flickered a pattern of his face as he drove.

'Come on and have a drink. We've the arrival of a baby girl to celebrate!'

Frances was glad of the brandy he poured. With a wry comment about his appearance he moved to ring up the farmer where he had been working earlier, assuring him he would be out soon. Frances replaced her glass and said she would run back to the farm, but Ian refused bluntly.

'I told Rupe I'd look after you, so I'll take you back.'

Meekly she followed him out to the car. Two minutes later she was back at the farmhouse and Jenny's scones were still smelling delicious. It was automatic for Ian to pick one up and munch it approvingly. Quickly Frances buttered a few and put on the kettle. Ian pocketed the scones and disappeared, not stopping for the tea. Frances felt oddly hurt, but later realised that he would have to work late trying to make up for lost time.

She had showered and changed before the phone rang. It was Rupe, his voice dancing as he told her that Jenny and the baby were both fine. 'They did a great job in the ambulance, Frances. The baby's hardly a pin-up girl, but Jenny and I think she's O.K. I've just rung through to Gam and the boys and they're tickled pink. Would you tell Ian I'll give him a ring tonight? And Frances, both Jenny and I want to say thank you.'

It had been arranged weeks before that Rupe would spend the first evening with old friends in town. His suitcase had been dropped there over Christmas as a precaution and now he would be glad of his spare clothes. Jenny would be pleased to have him so close at hand too.

Frances went back to Greytor, waiting in the stockyard under the shade of a willow tree. She whinnied indignantly, not used to being left, and Frances patted her as she swung herself up in the saddle. She was glad the water trough meant Greytor had at least been able to get a drink. She finished checking the stock, remembering too late about the feed paddock and the mob she had shifted out. Everything seemed fine, so she returned to the farmhouse.

Greytor rolled over on her back the minute the saddle and bridle were removed, rubbing herself in an abandoned frenzy. She then trotted down to the corner where the other ponies were feeding lazily. Frances decided she should take the ponies in turn for her morning rides.

She went for a swim, then ate her tea with an increased appetite. There were two programmes on T.V. she wanted to watch. The first was disappointing, but the second was rather good. It had just finished when the phone rang and glancing at the clock she saw it was nine-thirty.

'You O.K.?' Ian's voice sounded deep in her ear.

'Yes, of course,' Frances replied. 'Thank you for thinking of me, though.'

'I'll be at home if you need me. Goodnight.'

Frances heard the click as he replaced the receiver. She put down the phone feeling strangely warmed by his thoughtfulness. He had sounded so tired; perhaps he had just finished for the day. The conversation had been so brief, yet it sent her to bed at ten o'clock oddly content. When the phone rang early the next morning she answered it sleepily.

'Up you get, sleepyhead!' said Ian's voice. Her heart lifted as he inquired if she had slept well. Immediately thoroughly awake, she could hear the lazy humour in his voice, but she answered politely. He told her where he would be working and was preparing to ring off when she interrupted his farewell by inviting him to dinner. She knew Rupe would be home and she planned to cook something special. He agreed easily enough, saying he should make a point of finishing earlier that night.

As Frances went round the big patchwork of the flat fields that morning she planned the meal. She thought of some of her more exotic recipes tucked away in town, but realised that neither Rupe nor Ian would appreciate them after a hard day's work, so reluctantly she settled for simple food with fresh vegetables—fillet steak stuffed with mushrooms and served with golden chips and a side salad, then a dessert of pear Hélène. She had made the dessert before for Rupe and Jenny and Rupe had liked it. The recipe for the chocolate sauce was one Frances had developed after a lot of experimenting and she prided herself on it. The meal had the added advantage that she could prepare a great deal of it earlier. The steak could be grilled at the last moment. Once back at the house she pulled out mushrooms and fillet steak from the deep freeze and set them to thaw. Afterwards she poured some cooking wine into a dish and set the steaks to marinade. She peeled and chipped the potatoes, then cooked them, leaving them to drain all the oil out. In between she prepared a bean salad ready to pop into lettuce cups later. The pears were already bottled, so she reached down a large jar and made her chocolate sauce. There was always plenty of icecream in the refrigerator, so, satisfied she had done as much as she could, she tidied the house. She cut some more gladioli for the lounge, arranging the tall spears against a background of copper beech. A glance at her watch told her she had time for a swim, so she gladly changed and dived into the pool. She swam strongly for a few lengths, then slowed to a lazy crawl, until she finally floated, content to relax completely, keeping only a faint balance by adjusting her feet. When she climbed out she felt refreshed and relaxed. She pushed her wet hair back from her scalp and dried the worst off, wrapping another large towel round her as she went to shower and change. She put on a wrap as she blow-dried her hair into soft curls, letting it tumble loosely around her shoulders. She applied her make-up meticulously, wondering why her eyes seemed so green with excitement. She put on the jade cotton frock she had worn at Christmas, justifying it by telling herself they were celebrating tonight too. She clipped on the tree brooch Ian had given her, and looked at herself critically. Regretfully she sighed, knowing she was kidding herself. The men would come in covered in dirt and seeds and she would look ridiculous. Angrily she pulled on a pair of jeans and pulled off the pretty green frock. She tossed on a baby blue shirt with a wrap-over bodice that ended in a bow. Thoughtfully she pinned her silver tree to the centre and once again studied herself.

At least now she looked much the same as always, on the farm. The jeans were her best pair and did suit her and the blouse was a dress-up one too, but the men would hardly notice the difference, she thought regretfully.

She put some perfume on as a final touch and wandered out to the kitchen. A glance at the clock told her she had plenty of time. She wondered what time Rupe had arrived that morning. He must have been in and out again while she was down the back of the farm. Calmly she set the table in the dining room for three taking care to place each piece of cutlery carefully. She set out glasses, knowing that Rupe would insist on some drinks. Glad to have something to do, she polished the glasses till they shone, then wandered out to the garden. The swing couch stood rocking faintly so she sat down, easing her long legs up too. It was very comfortable if not very elegant, she thought idly. Somewhere a blackbird whistled a warning and Frances wondered what had startled it. Night was approaching slowly, the sunset in the western sky was a brilliant tangle of red, orange and gold. Soon Ian and Rupe would be returning, the noise of their motors would give her plenty of warning. For a few moments she daydreamed, allowing herself to imagine what it would be ike to be Ian's wife, watching for his return. She smiled, remembering the gentleness of his touch after the baby had been born. That golden side in his nature so obvious with Jenny, Rupe and the boys, yet she was shown only lightning glimpses rather as snow highlights a mountain.

A brief laconic greeting brought her out of her reverie. Startled, she swung her legs down, abruptly sitting in a more conventional pose.

'I'll put dinner on now. Sorry, but I was expecting to hear the car. Where's Rupe?' she questioned, struggling to keep calm.

'Rupe tried to ring you earlier, so he rang me. Apologies, etcetera, but he's staying in town tonight.'

Frances drew in her breath sharply, feeling sudden panic at the thought of Ian's company.

'Sorry, water baby, nothing's wrong. Jenny's fine, the baby's fine! I think Rupe just felt like staying in town another day. I didn't mean to worry you.'

Frances nodded. Ian had misunderstood the reason for her sharply drawn breath, but she was glad about that. She felt much safer talking about the family.

'What did Rupe say about the baby?'

Ian chuckled. 'You mean what didn't he say? I can give you height, weight, yells, opinions of doctors, nurses and even what the florist said. He's obviously enraptured!'

'So he should be! Wouldn't you in the same situation?' she said indignantly.

Ian stiffened. 'The situation won't eventuate. I don't intend to marry,' he finished curtly.

Frances looked at him, seeing him stare at her icily. She stood up and went to the kitchen. Ian chatted easily enough as she prepared the steaks and reheated the chips. Vaguely she realised he had been home and showered and changed into slightly more formal gear. His shirt was open though, and she could see the silver medallion shining brightly. Surely if she meant nothing he would not still wear it. The thought kept her going through the dinner. Everything had been cooked well but it could have been stale bread as far as she was concerned. She picked up the plates, rinsed them and stacked them in the dishwasher. Earlier the percolator had bubbled and Ian had taken it into the lounge along with the cups. Dimly Frances heard the television sound and she relaxed a little. At last now she could delay facing Ian. She cleared away the pots and pans, scrubbing them angrily as she thought again of Ian's words. She slammed the pots away and wiped down the bench. The kitchen gleamed and she had no further excuse to delay.

Ian was sprawled on the couch, his long legs angled easily. Casually he looked at her, then poured her a cup of coffee.

'Do you mind watching this? It's almost over,' he said.

'Of course not,' she replied. Actually she was glad he had switched on the television; at least now they didn't have to talk. She watched the last few minutes disinterestedly. It was a programme relating to growing crops as an alternative fuel source, so she understood Ian's interest. When it was over he stood up and politely thanked her for the meal. He asked if she wanted the television left on.

'Off, please, Ian.'

He flicked the switch. 'Did you hear from Gam today?'

'Help! I didn't even think to check the mail box. I'd better run out there now,' Frances replied with a smile.

'I'll come with you, then I can cut home round the road.'

They walked out together.

The house was set well back from the road. The trees whispered secrets in the softness of the wind. Overhead the lights of the stars glittered in the blackness of the sky. Frances caught her sandal in a stone and her balance wavered suddenly. She found a steadying hand on her arm, and replaced the sandal, glad of Ian's support. She was aware of his stiff rigidity beside her, as though he had been carved from the hard rock of the mountains. When they arrived at the letterbox Ian handed her a postcard, and by the light of the torch she held they read it together. The news of the baby's birth had been rung through earlier, but this card had been written before that event. As well there were one or two letters and Frances found one addressed to herself. She recognised Harry the photographer's handwriting immediately, and this would be a cheque for the last modelling job up on Victoria Park. Unthinking she kissed the envelope extravagantly.

'My goodness, the boy-friend's letter here and you hadn't even bothered to collect it! What a shame he can't see how you greeted it. Still, as I'm here I'll kiss you for him.' Ian gripped her savagely as she turned to leave. It was an angry, hard, demanding kiss that bruised her into response, but it turned then to a more gentle quest melting her agony. Frances drew closer, feeling the quick sensual replies of her own body.

Ian thrust her from him, the hateful, now familiar cold mask shutting her out. She did not attempt to speak, but gathered up the mail and turned and walked alone back up to the house. Aware in every cell of her body of the dark figure leaning against the mailbox, she finally reached the open door. Her heart was pounding and her mouth still suffered from the hard pressure of Ian's.

She tidied up the lounge mechanically, straightening up cushions, removing the coffee percolator, rinsing the cups. Finally she glanced at Harry's letter, and a wry thought made her stop for a moment. Could Ian have been jealous? It had been such a primitive kiss of angry passion. Frances remembered more clearly and realised that she was almost certainly right. The strange reaction they had on each other, the continual denial by Ian of love and marriage, yet his apparent inability to control his jealousy at the thought of Frances and another man. She knew that their lovemaking would be a natural blending. Physically they matched so well. Yet instinctively she recoiled from a purely sexual relationship. She loved Ian and wanted him to love her. She wanted to look at him with love and see him return the look. She wanted to smooth away the pressures and tensions when he was tired and for him to cherish her. She wanted to spend the rest of her life with him, having his children, being a part of him and he of her. Quite suddenly she knew that if she did not win his love her life would never hold the joy it was meant to have.

She poured herself a cup of coffee from the still hot percolator she had placed on the bench. 'My, I'm getting sentimental!' she smiled to herself. The problem was there, but she did not know how to handle it. If Ian did not love her there seemed to be nothing she could do. She jumped up and put away the coffee. Although it was quite late she knew she wouldn't sleep, so she started polishing the furniture. It was a job she had meant to do the next day. The furniture gleamed mirror-like with her efforts when finally she went to bed.

Early the next morning she rode out, not bothering to have breakfast. It was another fine day and all around her was full of a warm sunlit peace. At one stage she heard the roar of Ian's motorbike as he went round his farm. She waved an acknowledgment of his presence, then cantered on her way. It was one of the few times she had seen him, but she knew he must go round his stock early in order to have the rest of the day harvesting. When she did return to the house she found lunch quite enjoyable. She did vegetables and pulled a small casserole for Rupe from the deep freeze. It would be ideal for Rupert as tonight she was leaving, due for the weekend off. On Monday she would return early as Jenny should be sent home later that day with the new baby. She stayed at the farm until quite late in the evening making sure that everything was in the order Jenny liked. It was very hot, so she went for a swim before she left. The water soothed her and cooled her down. She showered and changed into one of her town dresses, then put her small suitcase into the Mini.

As she drove along the familiar roads electric cable poles flashed past as regular shadows. She noted their mast-like shape, the crossbars reminded her of a child's attempt at Christmas trees. The thick brown insulators looked rather like saucers with inverted cups balanced like decorations on each end.

Lines of trees and the odd farmhouse surrounded by trees helped split the landscape into patterns. In the distance Frances began to see Christchurch's Port Hills and in her rear vision mirror the mountains ran in a great line. The journey passed quickly as she skirted the centre of the city and drove direct to her home.

For once everyone was home and dinner that evening was a relaxed, happy meal. Martin had a girl-friend along and Kathy had brought along a pal from school too. Mr Elaman started playing the piano and soon everyone was joining in the songs. Then Kathy started on charades. They were an old family favourite game. No one wanted to break the fun up until it was quite late, and as she went to bed Frances was glad she could sleep in as long as she liked the next day.

By the time Monday morning came the lassitude of spirit she had felt over Ian had lifted and she was able to drive out to the farm with some of her former gaiety. She arrived early and was glad to read a note Rupe had left her. He told her that he would do the farm work that morning and would be going into town about half past twelve. Jenny would be ready at three, so he would have time to do a few things first.

Frances was very pleased. Now she could make sure the house was organised for Jenny's arrival. She found the washing basket and put the big machine on. While it was working she picked flowers and arranged them through the house. After the washing and the flowers she vacuumed quickly. Apart from Jenny and Rupert's bedroom and the lounge and kitchen, the house had a strangely unlived-in look. Normally the boys' toys and books had to be shifted. The boys were pretty good generally, but naturally there were times they forgot. Frances wondered how the holiday was going. She missed their gay conversation and bright presence in the house. As she worked she planned the dinner for that night. As it was cooler today she would make a cream of chicken casserole. She found a boiling chicken in the deep freeze and set it to thaw, then she selected a packet of mushrooms which had been frozen earlier, and peas.

When Rupe arrived to shower and change she stopped to give him some soup and toast for lunch. He thanked her for her efforts and said that Jenny and he had decided to give her a bonus. It was rather a nice gesture, thought Frances as she pocketed the cheque. She thanked him, feeling slightly shy about it, but realising the money would be useful for her trip. Her salary on the farm was not great, so this was a nice supplement.

After lunch she carried on with her work, straightening kitchen cupboards and drawers, and wiping them down. An hour before Jenny and Rupert and the baby were due she put on the casserole and peeled the potatoes and tender young carrots. She set the formal dining table with some care, using the heavy silver plate cutlery Jenny was fortunate to have. A glance at herself in the mirror showed her looking slightly tatty, so she showered and washed her hair, delighting in the spray of the water. She spent rather longer in the shower than she had intended, so she pulled on bra, pants and petticoat rather hurriedly. The casserole had to be turned down after its first twenty minutes or it would be tough. Frances flung a towel round her head turban-style and ran out to the kitchen. She pulled the casserole out, slowly added some more milk, then replaced it in the oven. Her hand switched down the temperature to very slow. Now she could safely leave it to simmer slowly. She turned to walk back to the bedroom.

'Hi, water baby!' The voice was deep and lazily amused. Its owner was framed in the doorway of the kitchen and dining room. 'Do you often do the cooking in that outfit?'

'Normally, no,' Frances replied coolly, deciding that hauteur was her best weapon. 'I'm sorry if I embarrassed you, but I didn't hear you come in. Excuse me while I get dressed, please.'

His bulk blocked the doorway and his eyes had a teasing light. She felt a thrill as he reached for her and caressed her bare shoulder. His kiss was gentle and brief. 'Go and get dressed.'

Her heart hammering, Frances slipped past him. She dressed quickly, endeavouring to quell the trembling his touch had aroused. As it was such a special occasion she felt she could dress up a bit. She put on a mid-calf length green satin skirt with a softer green satin shirt. A gold chain belt nipped in her waist. She hadn't worn it at the farm before as it was an exotic outfit more suitable for evening or cocktail wear. She clipped on the gold earrings when her hair was finally dry. All the time she was aware of Ian's presence in the lounge, but she was determined not to appear until her hair was dry. She had suffered quite enough with being called a water baby.

When she did appear Ian stood up and bowed. 'Mademoiselle, very chic.'

'Thank you, Ian,' she answered. He poured her a drink and she sat in one of the big deep chairs. Now she had time to study him she realised that he had dressed up too. She had become so accustomed to seeing him in his old working gear or just in shorts that her heart missed a beat. He looked devastatingly handsome, standing easily in his fine light shirt and long strides.

His eyes flicked up at her quickly and caught her studying him, and the amused glance he sent her made her grin cheekily.

'Just thinking what a handsome feller you are.'

'Keep thinking it!' he laughed, and handed her a plate of nibbles she had prepared earlier.

It was as well that they heard the car arrive then, the dogs barking in a frenzy of excitement. Both Frances and Ian went to meet them as Rupert proudly carried the new baby in. Jenny was hugged and kissed and the baby looked wide-eyed at the figures around her.

'I just finished feeding her in the car, so she can stay up for a little while. Here, Ian, hold her while I fix up the bassinet.'

Ian held the baby carefully, speaking softly, and Frances felt a pang at the tenderness in his voice. She went to help Jenny fix up the gear for the baby. When they returned Ian had the baby on his chest, its head snuggled into the column of his neck.

'It seems a long time since young Greg!' he smiled, handing the baby back to her mother.

'Have you decided on a name yet?' asked Frances.

'Not entirely. Rupert wants me to call her Jennifer, but with one of me around already I'm inclined to prefer something different. She looks such a sweet little angel now I'd like Angela, but think ahead how she'd hate me if she turned out like Ivan the Terrible,' Jenny chortled softly as they all laughed.

'I'd quite like Mary, after Mum,' put in Ian.

'You know, that's quite a nice idea,' said Rupert. 'Mary Marsden goes well together.'

'Mum would have loved it. I must admit I hadn't thought of that, but I rather like it,' added Jenny thoughtfully. 'Your mother was Ann. What about combining Mary-Ann, or even Marian?'

CHAPTER ELEVEN

THERE was discussion on this topic for quite some time. Rupert and Jenny were obviously quite pleased with the name, repeating it from various angles. While the discussion was going on Frances slipped out to the kitchen and served the soup she had made earlier. She sliced a cucumber decoratively on the side of each plate as a finishing touch. Rupert and Jenny put the baby to bed, then sat at the table. Ian helped her with the serving, then held her chair for her to sit down. She appreciated the thoughtful gesture and smiled her thanks. Conversation was mainly about the events of the past few days and the return of the boys at the end of the week. Ian spoke briefly about driving up to Nelson and staying with the boys for the last three days. Jennifer and Rupert both seconded the plan. Work for the season was going steadily ahead of schedule, thanks to the early start and Frances' presence on the farm.

The chicken casserole was delicious, and Frances was pleased to receive lavish praise from Jenny and Rupert. The creamy sauce had the subtle flavour of sherry with the merest hint of spice. The meat was juicy and tender. Although it was a big casserole there was only the empty dish to take to the kitchen afterwards, so obviously Ian had enjoyed it too. To complete the meal Rupert and Ian cleared away, insisting gallantly that the cook deserved a rest. They sat down in the lounge with coffee and liqueurs. Jenny seemed tired and Rupert said she had stayed up long enough. It was not long before the baby was due to be fed, so Jenny said goodnight. Rupert glanced at Ian and Frances with a sly grin and declared that he too would say goodnight.

Ian put on the record player and held out his hand to

Frances to dance. She moved into his arms with a bubbling joy delighting in his touch. The wine and the compliments had made her eyes sparkle and Ian, glancing at her, held her closer so that they seemed one being with the music. It was such a magic time, the gentle movement of her body reacting to the pressure of his, with the strange abandoned melting of her senses. The music bound them in silken threads and it seemed entirely natural to want the pressure of his mouth on hers.

Ian traced the line of her lips with a slow finger, reducing her to shuddering gasps. The kiss that followed shattered both of them. They separated and Frances looked at Ian. Even as she watched she saw the mask come over his features, shutting her out and making a mockery of that earlier kiss. For a glorious moment the earth had united with the sky, dazzling them both with ecstasy. They had been the only beings in the world for a moment of time. Now, still held in his glance, the fire had been turned to ice. Frances moved away before he rejected her again. Ian poured himself a drink and brought her one, but she refused it automatically as she felt quite numb already. Ian finished his drink slowly and Frances knew he was studying her. The tension in the room was overwhelming. She tried to control her feelings, struggling with her pride to help her. With an effort she said lightly, 'Ian, I'm going to say goodnight.'

'Coward!'

'Yes, I am. One moment you kiss me and I know you're the only man in the world for me, then two seconds later you're shutting me out.' She paused. 'That hurts, Ian.'

'Sometimes it's better to hurt you, then, honestly. I can't resist you. You carry the sun in your hair, the sparkle of the river in your eyes and the temptation of Jezebel in your body. I've never desired any woman as much as I want you. But you're not some girl for a night.' He laughed, a bitter, brittle sound. 'I think if we did sleep together I'd never be able to let you go.'

He stood in front of her. 'I'll get out of your way. This week I'm going to Nelson and after that I'll make sure I'm not around when you're here. February is always a busy time, so Rupert and Jenny won't notice.'

'I'm only hired till March the first,' put in Frances quietly. 'I go home every weekend, so you'll be quite safe to visit Jenny and the boys then.' A tear formed slowly in her eyes and glistened, trembling on to her cheek.

Ian caught his breath. 'Goodbye, Frances, my water baby.' He held her briefly, then moving aside, he strode from the room.

Frances reached the sanctuary of her bedroom. Mechanically she undressed, changing her good satin skirt and top carefully. It was only when she was in bed with her head buried in the pillow that she could allow the tears to fall. Never to see Ian again—the enormity of it swept her with desolation. Over and over his words came back to her, until finally exhaustion came and she slept.

CHAPTER TWELVE

THE sound of a baby crying woke Frances early in the morning. Dawn was breaking, shafts of apricot red and pink driving back the purple of the night sky. The sun would be up soon. Frances turned over in her bed. Her eyes felt sore and she felt as though she wanted to hide herself in the sheets. She closed her eyes and tried to sleep, but it was quite impossible. Already she had remembered that she would not be seeing Ian again. The agony in her heart had to be hidden. She groaned quietly. Reality was the sunrise, she thought as she pulled herself out of bed. She dressed in her old jeans and a neat check blouse. Her hair she brushed ruthlessly, pulling at it so it flattened to spring into long glinting curls. She wrapped a kerchief round it to hide its bright colour. Somehow, it seemed symbolic; she was there, head, face, arms, legs and body, but the flame of her personality was covered.

Breakfast was a staggered one. Rupert had his with Frances, Jenny stopping in bed to feed the baby. They went round the farm, and Rupert explained the week's feeding plans. At lunchtime they rode back to the house together.

Frances stayed on in the house helping Jenny with the baby. The baby was so tiny and helpless, her only protest a wail. Frances cuddled her against herself, holding the small bundle rather gingerly at first.

'I've not had much experience of small babies, I'm afraid!' she told Jenny.

'Lots of love and cuddling and you can't go far wrong!' laughed Jenny. 'Thad was very tiny when he was born, so we were inclined to handle him like a delicate piece of Dresden china. Everything had to be done to the minute, ready or not. With Ivan it was different. He was a big, bouncing bruiser right from the start. There was no chance of keeping to the clock where he was concerned. He yelled when he was hungry—and could he yell! As soon as he was fed he'd settle down as good as an angel. It was no good trying to tell him it wasn't dinner time for twenty minutes. By the time I'd had Greg, Rupert and I were both more relaxed about the babies. I guess he was lucky, really.'

'It's amazing how tiny the little one is. Look at her dainty fingers and the exquisite fingernails.'

The baby snuggled deeper into Frances' shoulder. She stroked the baby's back softly and rhythmically, while Jenny watched approvingly.

'See, it's quite easy. You've got the feel of it already.'

She felt strange emotions run through her when she saw the eyes of the baby looking back at her. Marian was obviously going to be very like her mother. Even now when she was so newborn Frances could see the outline of the face which reminded her so much of Jenny and Ian. Was this how Ian had looked as a baby? Unconsciously her hands held the baby firmer and she wriggled, fascinated by the bright hair peeping out. She was too small to clutch at it effectively, thought Frances. Later she helped Jenny to bathe her and that too was a joy.

When she was in bed that night Frances reviewed the day. If I take one day at a time, she thought quietly, I'll be able to manage. Soon her time at the farm would be over. She was glad she had the tickets for the cruise from the middle of March; it would give her a breathing space. While she was at the farm there was always a faint hope of seeing Ian. Once she had left she knew she would never see him again; the prospect seemed extraordinarily bleak.

At the end of the week she left for town, driving easily over the long flat roads. She knew Ian had been up to Nelson and would be returning with Gam and the boys on Saturday. Jenny and Rupert had asked her to stay on as Jenny was going to cook a special dinner to welcome them home again. Frances felt tempted to stay but did not wish to cause any embarrassment with Ian. The boys' reactions to the new baby would be a treat she would miss, and she was sorry about that. Still, there were the three weeks ahead, she reflected.

The weekend passed quietly. Frances' parents were away at a friend's bach at Kaikoura and Kathy was spending the weekend with a girl friend. Martin had some of his friends round and on Saturday night they had a small impromptu party. Frances thoroughly enjoyed herself, flirting outrageously with some of the boys. One of them had a guitar and he sang sweet love songs with a melancholy air. Inside, Frances could feel herself weeping in tune with the soft sadness. On top she was bright, vivacious and quite the life of the party. After everyone had left she cleaned up the room, opening windows wide and pushing chairs into their usual places. She washed the dishes and at last, with everything tidy, went to bed. Suddenly she felt as old as Methuselah, a condition which would have surprised her young companions, who thought Martin very lucky in having such a smashing sister. On Sunday night her parents returned late, so Frances made sure she was in bed early. Time enough to hide from their loving glances in the morning when all would be hustle and bustle.

When she arrived at the farm Jenny was just finishing bathing the baby. Incredibly she seemed to have grown just in the two days Frances had been away. For a little while they exchanged news then she read Rupert's instructions. There was quite a lot to be done, so she changed into her shorts and top immediately. She was tired when she fell into bed that night. It had been a hectic day. The three boys had greeted her with great Indian war-whoops followed by hugs and kisses. Afterwards they had helped her with the work. According to their mother they had wanted to get their baby sister on to a horse immediately, and there had been a fight among them for who should have the honour of giving Marian her first ride.

'Considering that their horses have scarcely been ridden for three weeks you could imagine my face! They know now not to put her near a horse till I say the word!' grinned Jenny.

'They seem very pleased with their new sister,' commented Frances. She held the baby close. The little baby smelt fresh and clean, her blue eyes looking around with wonder. The boys all wanted a turn at holding her too, so the baby was passed from one to the other with great care and tenderness. Ivan the Terrible was gentle and kind, more like Thad in his handling of the baby, while Greg sat a trifle anxiously but determined not to be left out of his turn. His smile of joy when the baby smiled at him was beatific. Jenny hastily removed the baby when a free fight was about to break out because Ivan claimed it wasn't a smile, just wind! The boys were hastily sent for a swim and Frances was glad to join them. At least now, she reflected, I can swim any time without feeling selfconscious about it. The boys had a race with her and she had to really struggle to keep up with Thad and Ivan. After five lengths Greg hauled himself out, content to watch. Thad won by the merest stroke and Ivan was just an arm-length away. Afterwards they sat on the side, bodies heaving, till their reactions steadied.

'I'll have to practise a bit more,' laughed Frances. 'I've got so used to just playing in the water I've got soft!'

'I beat Uncle Ian the first time.'

'So did I,' put in Ivan. 'After that he always beat us. We used to swim with him out to the raft most mornings and see who could get there first. It was really neat when Uncle Ian was with us.'

Jenny called them to change and have tea, and

Frances was pleased, as she found it difficult to listen to talk about the wonderful Uncle Ian! At tea the boys began talking about going back to school. The Christmas holidays with six weeks of freedom were over so quickly. The boys would be starting school in the morning; once more they would be flying out the door to run down to meet the bus at the gate.

The next day Frances waved goodbye to the three grey-clad figures, their shirts and shorts neatly pressed, socks pulled up, shoes polished, faces gleaming, hair wetly slicked down. They seemed to be anxious to be on time for once, no doubt looking forward to meeting their friends and telling each other about their holidays.

Thinking of holidays reminded Frances of hers, due so soon. Her lips curled into a weak grin as she remembered how she had bought it simply as a means of escape. Now it would be used for just that. She was to fly to Auckland and join the large luxury liner there. There would be three weeks in the Pacific cruising to Fiji and Samoa, then on to Sydney and back to Auckland. Strangely enough the trip held no joy for her now. Once she would have eagerly planned such a holiday, carefully working out outfits to wear, swimsuits and playsuits. Now the life seemed empty.

Greytor nickered softly and she drew herself back sharply to the matter in hand. The dogs had brought the sheep in from idly grazing and held them into a neat brown-coloured mob. Even the dogs knew what to do now without being told! Frances opened the gate and signalled to the dogs. Rupert had asked her to let this mob of sheep on to the lower flats. She sent Fay ahead to clear the way, restraining Scamp with a quick word. Once a wide enough path had been made with no danger of the mob mixing she led the sheep through. Scamp showed signs of becoming a really useful musterer, barking already at just the right moments. Frances watched as a couple of sheep decided to make a break for it. Scamp flashed past her in a wide semicircle and the two sheep, seeing their route blocked, rejoined the mob. Scamp trotted back, his bark ringing triumphantly, and Frances laughed. She praised him and Scamp looked at her, his mouth seeming to grin and his tail wagging. She closed the gate behind the mob and drove them to the far side where Fay and Scamp held them while she opened up the next paddock.

They repeated the manoeuvre until they got the mob down to the flats. From here the bank eased to the river, where this morning it glinted in the light. Frances took Greytor down in case he wanted to drink, the dogs had already raced in. They had wallowed and now were shaking themselves, sending a spray of diamonds flying in the sunlight. The beauty of the river always moved her, the colours of the water fascinating in their range. The stones were too hard to walk on to see the main bed of the river. At this width it was still some distance away. Ahead a couple of gulls screeched insults at their peace being disturbed. Frances pulled a drink from her saddlebag and perched herself against a big stone, using another for a backrest. It was a fabulous morning, the sun gleamed hotly, the wind had swung round to cool the air, the sky was blue. Towards the south Frances could see clouds lining up. With the wind springing up she knew there was a chance of rain. At the moment, though, it was pleasant resting against the sun-warmed rocks.

A startling zonk, zonk, zonk sound attracted her attention. This was echoed by another bird, and Frances realised she had disturbed two paradise ducks. She smiled softly. The ducks were obviously a pair, the female with her distinctive white head and neck being anxiously guarded by the green-necked male bird. Frances departed softly, telling the dogs to be quiet. The pair might have nested somewhere close at hand. She wondered if Rupe or Ian had noticed them before. She remembered her father telling her about the ducks as a child. There had been one female often to be seen on the Avon in Hagley Park in town. She knew a sadness for the bird as it had been obviously lonely, sometimes taking out its frustration on any ordinary wild ducks who dared to come too close. Her father had surmised that the mate had died, perhaps shot or savaged in some way. The bird seemed to make no attempt to seek its own kind, its own partial lameness possibly being the reason. Paradise ducks always mated for life, and this was the first pair she had seen out here.

At the top she remounted and glanced back. Now she understood the birds' alarm. Five small brown fluff balls waddled over the stones after the parent birds. They must have been carefully camouflaged from her sight. Somehow the day seemed a little brighter for the discovery.

When she told the family about the birds that night the boys were immediately anxious to ride down to the river to see for themselves. However, their mother suggested they wait for Waitangi Day.

'You can take a picnic and spend the day down there, but you stay right away from that section,' she cautioned.

Ivan agreed perhaps a trifle reluctantly, but they all cheered up when told they could borrow their father's binoculars. That night the wind blew sharply, driving rainclouds over the plains. After the heat of the preceding weather it was something of a shock to feel the coolness of the temperature. The rain began early in the morning and kept up a solid steady beat. The boys left for school, kitted out in oilskins and hats and gumboots. Frances was glad not to have to go out and even Rubert seemed happy to have a compulsory rest from the harvesting.

When the boys returned from school the rain was still steadily thrumming down. That evening Rupert listened to the forecast. If the rain was just as heavy in the hills the river would fill rapidly, all its tiny shiny strips merging to form one enormous, roaring brown torrent driving all in its path. In the morning the rain seemed to have increased its tempo slightly. The boys were sent off to school and Frances and Rupert discussed plans for shifting the stock to higher ground. 'Just to be on the safe side,' Rupert had smiled a trifle grimly. 'Summer floods can be disastrous. Thank God we harvested the white clover and the hay on the flats or we might have lost the lot.'

It was rotten work. Frances wore an old coat of Rupert's—Jenny dismissing her town coat out of hand with a wry laugh. It flopped wetly about her as she rode a decidedly bad-tempered Greytor. Her horse obviously thought they were mad to be out in such weather. The dogs walked behind them, even Scamp's tail was down flat and his coat wet. As they approached she could hear the river roaring and sucking at its banks. It seemed incredible to think that in such a short space of time it could have changed so much. She could see logs and bits of tree sailing rapidly downstream.

Gladly she turned her back on it, guiding the stock on to higher ground. The dogs were working steadily and Greytor too seemed to have realised the importance of the occasion. Rupert's distinct whistles could be heard even if she couldn't make out his figure through the rain. There was no danger to the stock at the moment, but if the rain continued at this rate the bank line in this low-lying paddock would soon be breached. The sheep were only too pleased to move to higher ground and Rupert slammed the gate shut behind them with a loud thump. Frances used her fingers to clear the rain from her face.

'I noticed Ian still has stock on his flat—we'll go and shift it for him. It's a wonder he isn't there already. He could be down further as he's got a bigger line of the river. O.K.?' asked Rupe.

Frances nodded. She was surprised how snug she felt inside the oilskin even if her face and hands were wet.

They had to go through the boundary gate higher up and then come down again to get on to Ian's land.

'Remind me to shift the toolbox later,' shouted Rupe, and Frances nodded. She glanced behind her. Surely Rupe didn't think the river would come this far, she reasoned. Sharp whistles sent her into action. Scamp streamed away, this time racing his mother in a wide cast. Ian had a lot of sheep down this side and they had to go over the ground to make sure none were missed. In the steady downpour that cut so much of visibility it was very difficult. When they had finished that paddock Rupert led on to the next and by the time they had completed it Frances felt rather worn. At one stage she heard the roar of Ian's motorbike in a neighbouring paddock—so he must be aware of them and glad of their help. Ridiculously she felt heartened just to know he was near. The next paddock, Rupert explained, was generally left to the last as the bank began to rise steeply so sheep could get to higher ground.

'We might as well clear it. Ian's still over the other ten-acre. Then we'll go back to Gam's and have a hot drink. Reckon we'll need it.'

Some of the sheep had begun moving to higher ground and Rupe went up to the cliffs to clear them while Frances went to open the gate. She was becoming chilled now and her ankle began to ache. She cleared the sheep on her side and as Rupe's still weren't through went up to see the reason for the delay. A couple of sheep skittered out of her way and she looked up, surprised. She could make out the big horse Rupe rode right at the end of the cliff. Its neck appeared to be arched over and its legs strained against some unseen force.

Desperately Frances called to Rupe. She wasn't sure what had happened, but obviously part of the bank had given way. She flung herself off Greytor and approached carefully, calling Rupe's name.

'Careful, Frances—stop there. The whole damn bank

may go!' Rupert's voice was urgent. 'I'm trapped by part of the landslide.' Looking down, she gasped in horror.

Rupe had one foothold on the bank and one hand firmly caught in the bridle of the horse. The bridle was trapped by a section of the cliff. 'Right, I'll get help! Hang on!' Which was a silly remark, she thought as she edged back. She spoke quietly to the big horse, shivers running along his muscles. While he held and the bridle held Rupert was safe. So long as the rest of the bank didn't give way and crash into the force of the river. Agonised, she wasn't sure what to do first. She knew there was a rope in the toolbox, but by the time she reached it, Rupert could have run out of luck. Dimly she heard the roar of the motorbike. She flung herself on to Greytor with a great deal more speed than elegance and raced the horse towards the fence. Not being familiar with the land, she guided the horse towards the sound. Obviously Ian hadn't heard her. A fence was coming up and there was no gate on this side. Deciding to jump it, she gathered Greytor evenly, then lifted herself as they cleared it neatly. Ian must have seen her, as he was speeding now to meet her. She reined in as he pulled up. Quickly she outlined the situation.

'Can you get the ropes from the box—if you jump it will be faster than me on the bike,' said Ian. 'I'll get down to Rupe.'

He roared away and Frances turned Greytor back towards the fence. Again they cleared it easily and she sighed with relief. The next paddock was becoming very puggy and she had a bad moment when Greytor slipped a little on impact. She pulled her along, relieved to feel the horse find her footing immediately. The next fence was taken easily and racing along they soon reached the box. Frances scrabbled at it, her fingers wet with cold, and the box proved hard to open. With a final click it opened, and she grabbed the neatly wound rope and a wire anchor pin. She loaded up the horse and set her again at the fences. It was a nightmare ride back to the spot, the rain lashing her directly and making the sight of the fences loom large. Frances thanked her lucky stars she had done a lot of jumping horses when a youngster. Arriving at the site, she could see Ian stroking the big horse, its muscles becoming rigid. Without raising his voice he told her what to do. She approached cautiously after tying one end of the rope to a tree as Ian had instructed. He took the rope and wire anchor and threaded it through, telling her to go back to the tree—'Hold on to the rope, darling, at least if the bank goes you'll be O.K.' She did as he said, then watched in anguish as he tied one part of the rope round himself then made a lasso of the other. She saw the loop fly over the bank and knew a moment of panic when the big horse reared and backed. If he caused too much motion the whole cliff could go, and Rupe and Ian would be killed unless they were very lucky.

Frances tore out, speaking quietly, knowing that she had to steady the horse. She had no way of knowing whether Ian's first lasso had caught Rupe or not. If it hadn't, it was doubtful if he had been able to survive the plunging of the horse. It seemed a lifetime as she reached the horse and stood on the edge of the bank, thankfully grasping the rope in one hand and stroking the frightened animal, its eyes white, rolling red in its head, its velvet muzzle crusted with saliva. She could see its fear easing as she softly leant against it, the contact with her body causing great shudders to rack it. She sighed with relief when she saw Ian pushing Rupert ahead of him and held out one hand, still calming the horse. As Ian clambered up and released Rupe from the stranglehold on his wrist Frances edged the big horse back slowly and softly, all too vividly aware that the least movement could trigger the slide further. Ian carried Rupert to a safe distance.

'Stay with him. I'll get the car.' He roared into the paddock and Frances flopped wearily down beside

Rupert. The horse had galloped off to the far side as soon as she released him, but Greytor stood patiently where she had left her. She called to her and was pleased when the mare came over to her. She reached into her saddlebag for a thermos of tea and held it to Rupe's mouth. He shuddered and gasped, the warmth shocking him, then drank thirstily. By the time Ian arrived he was sitting up, declaring himself fine, and it was only on his brother-in-law's insistence that he abandoned the horse to ride in the car. Frances wearily climbed on to Greytor and went to get the big horse, Duke.

So much for Ian's concern for her, she thought ruefully. She pulled Duke along, riding steadily in the rain after having neatly coiled the rope by the tree. The wire anchor pin could get lost, she knew it was easily replaced. Nothing would make her go on that dangerous ground. The fact that she had done so to save Ian and Rupe she pushed away from her. Duke moved slowly and she was glad to reach the outskirts of the paddock nearing the side wing of Coppers. Somehow she couldn't face Ian. She was heading on to home when Ian came driving out to her.

'Where do you think you're going?' His voice was angry. He reached for her, pulling her out of the saddle. Weakly she leant against him, conscious of his strength and her own need. He dumped her unceremoniously into the Land Rover, pulled the saddles and bridles from the horses and flung the gear into the back. The engine was gunned into a snarling roar and they lurched and bumped their way back to the house. He slammed the vehicle up to the back porch so she would not get wet. She laughed weakly, clad in the dripping oilskins, then he laughed too. Frances stepped down, feeling worn but slightly lighthearted, then removed her heavy outer gear. Amazingly she was still dry. Ian looked over her to make sure before unsnapping his own oilskins. Frances mopped her face with a tiny wisp of handkerchief from a pocket and Ian chuckled briefly. He pulled out a large one of his own and tenderly dried her face, outlining the edge of her eyes and lips.

Reaction was setting in now and Frances started to tremble. Ian gathered her against him, stilling her quivering limbs in the hard strength of his own body. She felt reassured and comforted. Then his mouth claimed hers in a tentative, gentle kiss.

'Come on, my love. Gam will have hot drinks ready for us.' He pushed her ahead of him and they walked into the kitchen.

Rupert was lying on the colonial couch along one wall. His wrist was strapped, but his colour was back to normal. Gam was sitting beside him feeding him with a hot whisky. She poured some of the heated drinks out for them and Ian passed a glass to Frances. When Rupert was more recovered he told them what had happened. 'A couple of sheep had gone towards the bank, so I followed them. They turned back and everything would have been O.K. if two great paradise ducks hadn't suddenly flown up practically right in front of Duke. He reared and over I went. The impetus sent that part of the bank flying and I grabbed the reins as it went. Thank goodness the reins looped themselves round my wrist or I would have been a goner! Then Frances came and she had the sense to get Ian and the rope. Come to think of it, where did you get that from so quickly?'

Frances explained briefly and Ian retold his part, then added how Frances had put herself at risk to quieten the horse when everything was so nearly lost. Gam listened quietly. When the explanations were over she said, 'Ian, the fire's going in the drawing room. Take Frances in there and I'll drive Rupe home.'

'Yes, ma'am,' answered Ian. He helped Gam get Rupert back to the Land Rover. Rupe appeared to have suffered no ill effects, but it would be necessary to run him to the doctor to check his swollen and bruised wrist: Ian rang Jenny and explained a little, making light of the danger.

'I should have gone!' put in Frances. 'I could have minded the baby.'

'They'll take the baby with them and Gam will go too. Much easier that way. Gam loves the wee lass, and she loves Jenny. Don't forget she's known her since she's been the same size.' He bent down and flung a large log on to the enormous fireplace and a shower of sparks flung up. Frances sank back in the couch and Ian wheeled it up to the fire, cutting off the rest of the room.

Frances felt warmed and relaxed. She was home. This would be another of those bitter-sweet memories to polish in years to come. Outside the greyness of the rain still steadily fell, forming a curtain to block off the trees and the farm around them. She looked at the fire dancing and flickering. The man beside her stared into the fire too, apparently lost in thought. The flames sent shadows chasing up and down the angles of his face. Frances studied him eagerly, delighting in the little highlights the fire revealed. He sensed her scrutiny and turned to her. He looked at her beauty, the red-gold curls glinting like polished copper in the flickering light, the pale skin showing the high cheekbones of her face, the soft red-lipped mouth, then his eyes were caught by the soft expression of love in her wide hazel eyes.

He bent to her, kissing her gently, feeling her instant response. Frances ached with longing, but already her heart told her to stop. She knew she could not bear the cold, shuttered look he would wear as once again he rejected her. She stiffened in his arms, dreading to look at his face. He held her closely, stroking her, calling her his darling. Frances dared a look at him. His face was full of light, and the expression in his eyes was a blaze of love.

Sighing softly with joy, she rested easily against him, offering her mouth for his kiss. There was a strange content and acceptance about it. Gone was the frantic searching, now they could be totally open to each other. The kiss deepened into a flame of fire which seemed to fuse them together.

Ian put her back gently on to the couch. 'Don't move, my darling!' He bent and kissed her fleetingly, then strode quickly towards his study. In a few moments he was back, a small box in his hand. He removed a ring from it. Tenderly kissing each finger until he came to the third finger of the left hand, he slipped the ring into position.

Frances gazed at him bemused, unable to fully appreciate the situation. She twisted the ring on her finger. It was a lovely old ring of two emeralds and two diamonds sparkling brilliantly like the flashing of water.

'Frances, I love you. Will you marry me?'

Frances noticed the strange shyness Ian seemed to feel.

'Oh, Ian, I love you!' She reached up and pulled the dark head down to her, kissing him hungrily. For some moments there was a silence in the room, broken only by the flare of the fire and the sharp sparks suddenly shooting. The brilliance danced on the emeralds and diamonds sending a band of colour as Frances cupped her hand around the dark curls of Ian's head.

'I take it that means yes to my proposal. My darling water baby! I've been such a blind idiot. I thought I was incapable of love for any woman and I nearly lost you. I saw you on the bank this morning when I knew that at any moment you might be swept away from me, then I realised that without you life would be like a desert without water. I love you, I love you, I love you.'

His kisses claimed her again, and it wasn't till the noise of the Land Rover disturbed the peace that they stood up again. When Gam came in her face lit up at the happiness she saw. Ian held up Frances' hand and the beautiful ring sparkled in the light.

'Ah, Mary's ring! I was beginning to think it

wouldn't see the light of day. You know how absolutely delighted I am.' She kissed Ian and Frances warmly.

'Welcome home, my dear! I know you'll be very happy here together.'

Frances, her hand in Ian's, looked towards the window. The rain had ceased. Amazingly the sunshine was already starting to struggle through the grey curtain. A sunbeam fell on their interlocked hands and they felt themselves blessed, the ring sparkling brightly in the light.

Harlequin Plus

THE ORIGIN OF THE HARLEQUIN EMBLEM

Have you ever picked up a Harlequin book and wondered about the figure in the diamond that appears on all our covers? He's Harlequin, of course, and this little fellow, wielding a baton and wearing a black mask and double-pointed hat, has a long and interesting history.

Although Harlequin has his origins in ancient Rome, it was in the sixteenth century that the character of Harlequin, as we know him today, emerged.

At the same time, groups of Italian actors formed traveling troupes called the *commedia dell'arte*. They roamed the countryside performing lighthearted plays filled with romance and comedy. The character of Harlequin was that of a servant or valet, and his role within the play was to provide comic relief. He accomplished this by performing an amusing array of antics and gymnastics. In fact, his very name is derived from the Italian word *arlecchio,* which means "always in the air."

Harlequin's role traditionally was one that combined humor with sadness and romance. Today, Harlequin has a similar role to play. From the covers of Harlequin novels, he invites millions of women to escape for a few hours into a world of excitement, laughter and love.

TAKE THESE 4
Harlequin Romances
FREE
as advertised on TV